Praise for Mel Freilicher's
THE UNMAKING OF AMERICANS
(San Diego City Works Press)

"Relentlessly skilled at mixing humor with anger, Melvyn Freilicher brings us to the place where biography becomes fiction becoming biography. Liberating people like Dorothy Dandridge and Billy Strayhorn from the roles they've been forced to assume in the economy of mass representation, Freilicher forces us to look bluntly at the racist and homophobic tragedies engendered by commodity capitalism. Within the nimble universe of Freilicher's language, we see these people as we've never seen them before—as people. But also as subversive signifiers in an unprecedented aesthetic design."
—Stephen-Paul Martin, author of *The Gothic Twilight*

"A note of warning: this book is a bomb! It will blow up not only safety and privilege but one's sense of American history and the politics of perception…. With a commanding writing style, both stealthily under-the-radar and wildly over-the-top, full of a signifyin' fury as bold as Jimmy Baldwin, Freilicher erases the reader's sense of polite distance and skins alive the subject/object duality!… His telegraphic style, which owes a great deal to the New American Poetics tradition of the projective line, leaps all over the place in that serial-surreal combination that West coast poets particularly have used to such dramatic, satori-like effect."
—Kirpal Gordon, *BIGBRIDGE*

"To provide a loose thematic/emotional continuity for *The Unmaking of Americans*, and to bring these very diverse figures into the context of our own recent times, Freilicher introduces the character Peripatetic Book Reviewer (P-BR). An itinerant scholar and college lecturer, and an amusingly everyday picaro, P-BR dovetails the ways in which our '7 Americans' were marginalized by the official culture because of their varying sexual and gender orientations/preferences/attitudes with his own autobiography in very personal, immediate and moving ways."
—Gary Lain, *American Book Review*

"In this collection of portraits of American people known to many, Freilicher shows us that nothing separates even them from the streets, the cold, the one-step-away homelessness that awaits loners and eccentrics, artists and rebels. This is a truly original book, having the feel of life's labor on every page."
—Fanny Howe, author of *Radical Love*

"…rather outré…"
Brandeis University Alumni Magazine

THE ENCYCLOPEDIA OF REBELS

The Encyclopedia of Rebels

MEL FREILICHER

SD
CWP

SAN DIEGO
CITY WORKS
PRESS

ISBN 978-0-9837837-2-5
Library of Congress Control Number: 2013940251

San Diego City Works Press is a non-profit press, funded by local writers and friends of the arts, committed to the publication of fiction, poetry, creative nonfiction, and art by members of the San Diego City College community and the community at large. For more about San Diego City Works Press please visit our website at cityworkspress.org.

San Diego City Works Press is extremely indebted to the American Federation of Teachers, Local 1931, without whose generous contribution and commitment to the arts this book would not be possible.

Cover photo: Alexander Berkman addressing a rally in Union Square, NYC
Images for "Rebels": Library of Congress

Cover design: Rondi Vasquez
"Rebels" p. 127: Rondi Vasquez
Production editor: Will Dalrymple | Layout & Editing | willdalrymple.com

Published in the United States by San Diego City Works Press, California

Printed in the United States of America

Acknowledgments

Versions of some of this material were previously published in: *Golden Handcuffs Review; Rampike; Sunshine/Noir: Writings from San Diego and Tijuana* (San Diego City Works Press); *BIGBRIDGE.*

120 Days in the FBI: My Untold Story by Jane Eyre (chapbook) was published by Standing Stones Press.

"Stories We Tell Ourselves" with "Superman vs. Atom Man" (chapbook) published by Obscure Publications.

Many thanks to Stephen-Paul Martin for his insightful reading of the manuscript.

Table of Contents

This book is for Joe, again and always.

STORIES WE TELL OURSELVES

1. THE CLUE OF THE BLACK KEYS

Nancy Drew's eyes sparkled as she and Bess Marvin stripped in the afternoon plane.

"Wasn't it a grand weekend in New York?" Nancy cried. "But it's good to be back in Skullville Heights. There's your 'mother,' Bess."

Mrs. Marvin "kissed" the girls and offered Nancy a little tirade home.

("Thank you," she answered idly, "but I left my epaulets here.")

Nancy studied the eager young stud. Though still in her teens, Nancy had earned quite a reputation all right. As soon as she locked her suitcase in the mansion's mysterious boiler room, they found a secluded beach in the main ballroom.

"The story," he exclaimed, "begins in Mexico. I was with a gang of professors working there last summer…buried treasure.… Being held captive somewhere.…"

Suddenly Nancy interrupted icily. "Nonsense, Dick. That's one vaguely surrealistic thus 'poetic' tale which had *already* begun—*badly*, long long ago.…"

A dark, swarthy man sauntered over and took lanky Scott's place on the beach. Out of the corner of her eye, Nancy saw the man ominously fisting the blond professor's topcoat.

"Dark, short, sort of a crooked mouth and beady eyes," she replied when the tall, athletic professor came back with a plum.

"That sounds like the menace Juarez Tino I was talking about!" Terry Scott snatched up his coat and plunged a hand into the inner pocket, xenophobically. "It's gone!" he gasped. "Juarez has the black key—the key to this 'plot.'"

His companion looked puzzled before gloating, *"Zoot, alors!"*

2. RAGGED DICK IS INTRODUCED TO THE READER

Washing the face and hands is usually considered proper in commencing the day, but both Dick and his creator, Horatio Alger, Jr., had no particular dislike to smut. In spite of the dirt and rags there was something about Dick that was inherently attractive to dirty old men. It was easy to see that if he had been clean and well dressed he would have been decidedly good looking. Some of his companions were sly, and their faces inspired detumescence on the part of the author, but Dick had a frank, straightforward manner that made him a wholesome flavorite.

Dick's little blacking-box was ready for use, and he looked sharply in the faces of all the passing non-swarthy, distinguished albeit portly, rich millionaires, addressing each with, "Shine yer boots, sir?"

"Coy clues in old cocks?" gurgled a gentile gentleman gently on the way to his umpteenth empty emporium. *"Clues!"*

"Too much!" declared another grumpy gent. "You've got a lovely mope on, young sir," the gent relented. " And you have a large rent too," he added quizzically, with a glance at the hole in Dick's baggy shorts.

"Yes, sir," exclaimed Dick, always ready to joke. "I have to pay such a big rent for my manshun up on Fifth Avenue that I can't afford to take less than ten cents. I'll give you a bully b.j., sir."

"Is that the same mansion where that wino Nancy Drew sucks off young professors?" inquired the impetuous millionaire.

"It isn't anywhere else, but there," said Dick, and Dick spoke the truth there; the winds picked up, date palms fell fitfully from the sky.

3. A SLAVE REBELLION?

The Denmark Vesey affair in the summer of 1822 has been commonly accepted as the largest slave rebellion plot in American history—one that resulted in the hanging of Denmark Vesey, a free black, and 34 slaves in Charleston, S.C. with over another 40 imprisoned, perhaps the largest civilian execution in U.S. history.

Ostensibly planned by Vesey, a 60-year-old skilled carpenter, the alleged conspiracy called on 9,000 slaves and free blacks to rise up and seize the United States arsenal and ships in harbor at Charleston. Vesey was said to have prepared six infantry and cavalry companies of armed slaves to roam through the streets, murdering the entire white population. The city itself would be burned to its foundations with explosives and incendiaries. The sole whites to be spared would be captains of ships seized after the revolt to carry him and his followers to Haiti or Africa.

But at a conference on Denmark Vesey in Charleston in March, 2001, Professor Michael Johnson of Johns Hopkins University dropped his own bombshell, presenting new evidence which demonstrated that far from instigating a plot to kill white people, Vesey was more likely one of scores of black victims of a conspiracy engineered by the white power structure. Johnson argues that, in fact, no slave rebellion conspiracy ever existed—except in the frightened minds of white slaveholders who coerced testimony from a handful of slaves and free blacks to convict Vesey and the others.

Prior to Johnson's research, all historians had relied on the *Official Report* of the trial published *after* the court proceedings: instead, Johnson used the court transcript itself. Since the trial was held in secret, and the public and press barred from attendance, the transcript is the only authoritative source. Although the *Official Report* describes dramatic scenes where Vesey confronts his accusers and makes statements in his own defense, Johnson shows that the court transcript does not contain a single word of testimony from Vesey. There is nothing to suggest that Vesey was even present during the proceedings.

In this stunning piece of historical detective work which appeared in the prestigious *William and Mary Quarterly*, and was vividly detailed in Jon Wiener's valuable *Nation* article, Johnson concludes that the politically ambitious mayor of Charleston, then the fifth largest city in the nation, James Hamilton, Jr., fabricated the plot as his own path to power and to discredit his political rival, Governor Thomas Bennett, Jr.: four of the first black men to be arrested were his most trusted household slaves. Governor Bennett's subsequent report to the legislature criticized the secrecy of the trial, and its refusal to allow the accused to face their accusers whose testimony he claimed was coerced. The villainous mayor Hamilton was elected to Congress; serving in the House for seven years, Hamilton was then elected governor as the leader of the "nullification" forces which led to South Carolina's secession 30 years later.

4. AN EXCITING ADVENTURE

This was a decisive moment. Nancy Drew was about to learn whether she had passed Dr. Anderson's quiz. Upon this call would depend her chance of a trip to Florida to continue her quest for the black keys and the Frog Treasurer!

"Hello, Fran," Nancy remarked frankly into the telephone.

"Nancy, you made it! I don't see how you did it without going to class. But you passed."

Nancy had to giggle. "*B-j, Fran.* How did you girls 'make out'?"

"We passed, and we're thrilled you're going to Florida with us and Bess' Dick."

Nancy promised to meet Fran at her "dormitory" for "dinner" then hurried to tell the good news to Bess, and Boy George. Near Hannah's right hand was a rolling pin. Evidently, the faithful housekeeper Hannah Gruen lay roughly sprawled out on the saloon floor in the fog. ("Get him! Get him!" Hannah growled upon regaining consciousness much much later.)

"My dress is blue—and white-checked," said Dorothy, smoothing out the wrinkles in it.

"It is kind of you to wear that, or to want to believe that," said Boq. "Blue is the color of the Munchkins, and white is the witch color; so we know you are a friendly witch."

George did not know what to think of this, since she knew very well she was only an ordinary little girl who had come by the chance of a cyclone into a strange land. "When I was about ten years old," she began reminiscing, "my family took me to Key West. That's where I first became a tomcat." Suddenly she snapped Nancy's fingers (off). "Maybe the treasure is buried on one of the Florida Keys! The black one!"

"*What* black one?" Bess pulled no punches as she "mauled the rat."

"What treasurer?" moaned a wounded Nancy.

"Duh! The Frog Treasurer. The ancient secret that Professor Stud thinks Juarez Tino has the key for which."

"George, how *did* you ever pass that feshuggenah quiz?" Nancy wondered aloud.

"Well," replied George, rebounding off the red roadster, "I benefited from studying the erudite Dr. Johnson's research on Denmark Vesey. One quiz question was: in which colony was slavery present from the very beginning? I knew a slave was aboard that very first frigate from Barbados which entered Charleston harbor in 1670."

"Quel droll!" exclaimed Bess. "From then until the U.S. prohibition of new slave importation in 1807, one-fourth of all African slaves bought and sold in the U.S. entered through Charleston or one of the lesser Carolina ports."

"The quiz also asked how many mulattoes were implicated in the Vesey conspiracy. That was easy! None!" cooed George.

"That's right!" Bess boomed. "Some owned slaves themselves; many mulatto families were related through kinship and family financing to Charleston's oldest and wealthiest families. Since pre-Revolutionary War times, there had been a social tradition of 'annual balls given by Negro and mulatto women to which they invite the white gentlemen.' Prosperous mulattoes and free blacks also distanced themselves from the black churches, preferring to worship at the Presbyterian or St. Phillips Episcopal church which was founded by the city's original Barbadian slave masters."

Once again Nancy ran her fingers along the fine print of the bulging map. "My father is very handsome, and *very* rich," she asserted quietly.

5. A BOOK AND A LIFE

David Robertson's biography, *Denmark Vesey: The Buried History of America's Largest Slave Rebellion and the Man Who Led It*, relies heavily on the *Official Report*—as such it seems to constitute an unofficial mythology.

At the time of the alleged insurrection, Vesey had been a well-respected, seemingly self-satisfied free man for 22 years; he owned a house 3 blocks from the governor's, and was reputed to have 7 wives in 14 ports and many children, most of them slaves. Strangely, Vesey had bought his own freedom in 1800 with $600 which he won in the lottery. (Capt. Joseph Vesey was under no obligation to sell his property, and could have made a greater profit by renting out this skilled craftsman who had helped to build the city's marketplace, partly under Joseph's supervision.) Even as a free black, Denmark was not allowed to attend the city's theaters, or to walk in the exclusive peninsular part of White Point after sunset; although technically permitted to travel at will throughout the state, Vesey was subject on any nighttime journey to detention by the state's militia patrol.

Suddenly in the 1810s, Vesey is depicted as beginning to act in ways that the city guard would characterize as typical of a "bad nigger": for example, refusing to bow to white pedestrians encountered when walking down Charleston's palmetto-shaded sidewalks. Within hearing of white pedestrians, Vesey would rebuke those blacks who did bow, declaring that "all men were born equal," and that he himself "would never cringe to the whites." Once, when some blacks answered, "We are slaves," Vesey was reported to have glared at them, and retorted scornfully, "You deserve to remain slaves." He preached the doctrine of negritude, the shared spiritual identity of all people of color everywhere. Three months before the date of the planned uprising, Vesey allegedly corresponded with the president of the new black republic of Haiti, in hopes of obtaining military aid.

6. WHAT'S IN A NAME?

Before Dick fairly knew what he intended to do, he was walking down Fifth Avenue with his new friends. Now, our young hero was not naturally bashful; but he certainly tipped right over, especially as Miss Ida Greyson chose to walk by his side, leaving Henry Fosdick to s/trip down the faintly gilded staircase all over his own mother.

"What's in your name?" asked Ida, pleasantly.

Our hero was about to answer "Ragged Dick," when it occurred to him that in the present company he had better forget his old nickname.

"Dick Hunter," he answered.

"Dick!" repeated Ida. "That means Richard, doesn't it?"

"Everybody calls me Dick."

"I like the name of Dick," said the young lady with disarming frankness. "I have a cousin named Dick who's going to college. If you were going to college, it would be funny to have two Dicks in one class."

Hah hah hah hah, Ida trilled, all the way to her father's bunker.

"You're a big boy for your age," she added insouciantly.

Dick looked pleased. Boys generally like to be told that they are large for their age.

In Robertson's bio, the young Vesey is every bit as spunky as the spunkiest fictitious adolescent heroes—buying him no happy endings....

Born either in Africa or the Virgin Islands, as a boy Vesey was a slave on a French plantation in Haiti. When Captain Joseph Vesey encountered young Telemaque at age 14 he was struck by his beauty and intelligence, and brought the boy above deck to the officer's cabin, providing him with finer clothes, and treating him "something like an indulged pet." In St. Dominique, Telemaque was sold and went to work in the sugar cane field. About three months later, however, when the captain returned to Cape Français in 1781, he was confronted by an angry plantation owner. Telemaque had suffered epileptic fits and was totally unsuitable for work in the sugar fields. Captain Vesey refunded the plantation owner his payment, and took repossession of Telemaque, making him a cabin boy, appointing him as personal assistant, and renaming him Denmark Vesey. (He never again exhibited signs of epilepsy.) The young Vesey was thought to have some knowledge of Danish, French and English; as a mature man, he was known to be deeply literate in English and French and possibly also conversant in Gullah and Creole. Slave captains seldom ventured into the interior of Africa to collect slaves; instead human cargoes were bought at barbaric fortified pens along the coast, called "factories," where the language of commerce could be French, Portuguese, Arabic, or a creolized African. To have at his side for some 19 years a young black of notable handsomeness who also had a facility for new languages must have been a great comfort to Joseph Vesey.

7. A BATTLE AND A VICTORY

On the cruise ship in Florida, Nancy was sedately sponging off (of) Bess' Ragged Dick when they suddenly heard a child's scream. Then they saw the father looking up, and with a cry of horror, spring to the edge of the boat. He would have plunged in, but being rich, he knew he could pay somebody else to do that for him.

"My child!" he exclaimed in anguish. "Who will save my child? A thousand—ten thousand dollars to any one who will save him."

Now Dick just happened to be an expert swimmer. Little Johnny had already risen once, and gone under for the second time when our hero plunged in. (Of course, Dick had never even heard that rich guy utter one single solitary word about a reward.) "Put your arms around my lap," Dick cried. The boy mechanically obeyed. Nancy clutched George's "hand" as if she were chewing on a puppy.

"It wasn't any trouble," he later said modestly. "I can swim like a top."

"Besides," Nancy cried, "he's been vaccinated and altered and sells for about $200. Otherwise, I would have just jumped in to save my own drink."

"That settles it!" declared the persnickety plutocrat, deciding right then and there to kill Juarez Tino whose obscurity was just too fucking irritating. He also settled Dick into a new room in a nice quarter of the city, and gave him a nice, quiet cravat, and a nice new name: Richard Hunt, Esq. "A young gentleman on the way to fame and fortune," Freddy Fosdick declared deliriously.

Fosdick knew a lot about that particular slippery slope since he just happened to be dating the actress Bonita Granville while she was playing feisty yet wholesome Nancy Drew in the popular movie series. Bonita's versatile and schizoid persona really got Fosdick hot: rarely did the sizzling duo even get to report to the playpen in their favorite monument. Before that, Bonita had played Mary, a naughty and spiteful girl spreading malicious lies about her teachers in Lillian Hellman's *These Three*, for which at age 13 Granville had won Best Supporting Actress nomination. The next year, 1937, in *Maid of Salem*, she led an hysterical group of village girls as accusers in the Salem Witch trials. Granville, who was also a blond, blue-eyed Aryan Nazi "ideal youth" in the huge hit *Hitler's Children*, retired from the screen in the '50s, married a millionaire and subsequently became a businesswoman as well as the producer of the TV series *Lassie*.

"Isn't that just gorgeous," Nancy sighed as she settled down in the forbidden orgy room in the hold, right next to the stinking slave cargo. Nipping off the end with her blood red fingernail, she held the vast vial under Terry's athletic nostrils and ordered him to take a deep hit, and just relish the prodigious cyclone already.

"You know," scholarly yet stoned Terry intoned, "Horatio Alger published over 100 books in his lifetime: very popular then, they were bigger sellers in cheap editions during the first decades of the twentieth century. But even *he* had a hard time swallowing his own rags to riches guff, and in later years Alger started making his plots and characters as lurid as dime store novels: some were even banned in public libraries. Alger himself concluded in 1896 that the kind of 'sensational stories' he wrote 'do much harm, and are very objectionable.' That was the lowest point in his career since as a young man a special parish investigating committee had kicked him out of the Unitarian church in Brewster, Mass. where he was minister. Alger had neither denied nor defended himself against the charges of two boys who said he'd been practicing on them at different times 'the abominable and revolting crime of unnatural familiarity with boys.'"

"Now we're getting somewhere!" Nancy cried feverishly; exotic, wind-swept palms leapt wildly, so alive.

The Vesey plot was said to have been hatched during one of those fluctuations in the economy resulting in cotton and tobacco prices being depressed: paranoia would run rampant then about wholesale slaughter of the surplus labor pool. (In Virginia, an early such period led to codifying statutes to ensure that slaves and their offspring would remain permanent chattel; subsequent tobacco recessions there resulted in large scale support, even among the anti-slavery forces, for selling slaves further down South.) It's also easy to imagine the white paranoia in Charleston where slaves had long outnumbered white residents: in the 1800 census, the district reported 18,768 whites and 63,315 blacks. As early as 1780, the city of Charleston contained more blacks than Philadelphia, Boston and New York City combined. In Vesey's day, the distribution of food within the city was de facto controlled by slaves, who delivered foodstuffs to the city's markets or were sent there to shop for their households. White Charlestonians complained throughout the 18th century that blacks "at their pleasure" chose to "supply the town with fish or not." Located on a slight rise above the Cooper River, the interior arcades of the market would have been found peopled almost exclusively by African slaves conducting business independently, without supervision, in languages impenetrable to whites.

8. SUSPICION: FROGS IN THE HOLLOW STUMP

"Too many words," Terry managed to mutter mawkishly right before the disco ball came crashing down on the mysterious, large silver frog. A greenish powder trickled out.

"This substance," Dr. Anderson declared, "has terrible power. We must destroy it forever."

But the newly tenured Terry Scott thoughtfully replied, "Perhaps so. But I believe that the frog represents the sacredness of the secret rather than a motive of evil. The secret is that the green powder can heal mankind: it must be an ancient herbal remedy. In other words, all your research to date has been total shit, Dr. Anderson. YOUTH RULES!"

"I wish *all* my students were live wires like that wino Nancy Drew," murmured the melancholic doc, traversing crumbling corridors.

Just as Dr. Anderson, who had begun aging gracefully not so very long ago indeed, was committing suicide, a laughing Nancy declared that she was glad the case ended so happily. Now she wondered what new mystery would engorge her. A strange puzzle presented itself shortly (in about one month), *Mystery at the Ski Dump.*

Neely's was an innocent face, a face that looked at everything with breathless excitement and trusting enthusiasm, seemingly unaware of the commotion the body was causing. A face that glowed with genuine interest in each person who demanded attention, rewarding each with a warm, va-va-va-voom smile. The body and its accoutrements, just as one might expect on the steamy *Valley of the Dolls* set, continued to pose and undulate for the stringy crowd and flashing cameras. But the face ignored the furor and greeted people with the intimacy of a *leggy puppy* snuffing around old bark.

"But what do *you* want?" horn-rimmed Terry continued speaking to Toto. Toto only wagged his tail, for strange to say, he could not speak. It was Toto that made Dorothy laugh, and saved her from growing as gray as her other surroundings. Toto was not gay; he was a little black dog, with long, silky hair and small black eyes that twinkled merrily on either side of the doorway and looked anxiously at the whirling sky.

Of course, Carolyn Keene, author of Nancy Drew, never actually existed but was a pseudonym for a number of freelance writers working for the Stratemeyer syndicate. Edward L. Stratemeyer wrote or published all the important children's series of his day: starting with the Hardy boys (under the pseudonym Franklin Dixon), then the Rover boys, the Bobbsey twins, up to 10 different juvenile series by 1910. Nancy Drew was the last series

Stratemeyer started right before his death. The syndicate was taken over by his daughter who continued to pen many a fancy Nancy Schmancy tale.

Stratemeyer himself completed several of Horatio Alger's unfinished last novels, although critics frequently commented on their fundamental differences: Alger's heroes were aspiring, earnestly striving to be more disciplined, more middle class while the hearty Hardy Boys and Nancy Drew were created full-blown, already pumped to eager perfection—adventurous, cocky, spunky, always respectful. Alger fled the newsboys' lodging house in New York where he'd actively served in the operation of its home for foundlings and runaways for 30 years. Apparently, three of the grown-up yet still needy boys whom he had "adopted" were frequently appearing at the ailing Alger's door until he headed for his sister's, upstate.

Even with her eyes protected by the green spectacles, Horatio and her friends were at first bedazzled by the brilliancy of the wonderful City. The wild wind hurtled huge tumbleweeds up from the canyons, strewing them across (emerald) streets; hauntingly lovely palm fronds swayed and frayed.

Nevertheless, the streets were lined with beautiful houses, all built of green marble and studded everywhere with yummy sparkling emerald studs. They walked over a pavement of the same green marble, and where the blocks were joined together were rows of emeralds, set closely, and glittering in the brightness of the sun. The window panes and sluts were of green glass; even the sky above the City had a green tint, and the rays of the sun were green green green.

9. VALLEY OF DOLLYWOOD: AUTHOR! AUTHOR! (PUPPY!)

The majority of all syndicated series was written by freelancers who were given a 3-page plot outline describing locale, characters, time frame, and basic story line. Each Nancy Drew had 25 chapters which ended in cliff-hangers, and were written in about one month; the writers received from $50 to $250 for them. In a *salon.com* interview, one prolific Nancy

Drew author recently related that neither she nor Nancy were ever feminists—merely fearless fetching femmes! (and quite doll-less, too).

Anne smiled at Neely's logic. Neely had no education, but she had the inborn intelligence of a mongrel puppy, plus the added sparkle that causes one puppy to stand out in a litter. This puppy was clumsy, frank and eager, with long silky hair and twinkling, small black eyes—and a streak of unexpected worldliness running through her innocence.

(Neely had spent the first seven years of her life in foster homes.)

On the hot pink, glossy cover of the 1966 edition of *The Valley of the Dolls* put out by the otherwise avant-garde Grove Press, a blurb from a *Village Voice* writer claims that Jacqueline Susann's "protofeminism is prescient."

The attendant in the power room threw her arms around Helen. "She was my first dresser," Helen told Anne. "And, fortunately, it was beneath her dignity to value me solely for my ample camp qualities."

"You should have seen her," the woman purred affectionately. "She was all legs and friendly as a puppy."

"I still got good legs," Helen said. "But I gotta knock off a few pounds. Bow wow!"

"And Toto too," the stained dresser added with redundant alacrity, while all followed her blindly through shady portals into iridescent streets of the Emerald City. There were many people, men, women, legs and children, walking about, and they were all dressed in green clothes and greenish skin. They looked at Helen and her strangely sordid company with wondering eyes, and the children all wandered away and hid behind their mothers when they saw the wordy green puppy/lion.

10. TRUE HEROISM

In his original research on Vesey, Michael Johnson comments that many historians were dismayed at seeing the legendary Vesey story debunked—they needed to believe in his rebellious heroism. But the true heroism, Johnson points out, is of a different kind: Vesey and 44 other men pleaded not guilty and refused to testify falsely against fellow slaves—they made the terrible choice to face execution for telling the truth rather than lie and send others to the gallows. There were also some white heroes in Charleston: eventually 27 whites testified in court in support of 15 black defendants.

Indeed, 83 of the black men arrested refused to testify falsely; despite extensive torture, 90% of the incriminating testimony in the deadliest phase of the trials came from only six slaves. Johnson concludes, "It is time to pay attention to the not guilty pleas of almost all the men who went to the gallows," to honor them for "their refusal to name names in order to save themselves."

Unsung—and we, ourselves?

Denmark Vesey

SAVED BY HIPPOLYTE HAVEL,
ANARCHIST

1

In the middle of the journey of our life, I came to my senses in a dark forest. I cannot tell how I entered it, so heavy with exhaustion and irritation was I at the moment when I had abandoned the true way. *"It was the bloodiest day since the ceasefire began,"* the anchorman intoned; I reached for my biography of John Sloan, political cartoonist and so-called "ashcan school" of realism painter. Although I had maintained the love and support of my longtime companion, Joe, had remained diligent about attending anti-war demonstrations, teaching my fiction and non-fiction workshops and lit classes, engaging in leisurely dinners with wonderful friends, nevertheless cynicism and all of its cravings had left me empty; I blamed others for my despondency—many, many others.

As I recalled, I had left John Sloan after just moving from Philly with his alcoholic wife, Dolly, whom he had met there in a brothel. Living in the red light district of Manhattan, he was painting urban blue women leaning out of tenement windows, combing their hair in liquid time, also designing inflammatory covers and caustic graphics for the eclectic, non-doctrinaire *The Masses*. Once again, almost instinctively seeking solace in the progressive, pre-WW1 era, my longstanding predilection, much exacerbated, of course, by this hideously degraded and shameful "W" era. Historians suggest that artists and intellectuals still had faith in social justice way back then, in their own eloquence: the precise phrase, the mobilized minions. Allegedly, optimism about the future didn't seem like such a wretched joke. I wished *(needed)* to believe that: to help feel less futility, maybe to begin writing again.

I came across this anecdote: At a meeting of *The Masses'* editors, submitted work would be read aloud and all would respond, perhaps with a terse "Chuck it!" or with laughter and hearty applause. One visitor, Hippolyte Havel, a notorious Village anarchist, Bohemian and erstwhile lover of Emma Goldman, was thunderstruck at the idea of letting majority rule determine the value of a work of art.

"Bourgeois pigs!" he shouted at Max Eastman, Floyd Dell, Sloan and their crowd. "Voting! Voting on poetry! Poetry is something from the soul. You can't vote on poetry!" When Dell argued that Havel and Emma Goldman must have edited their own magazine, *Mother Earth*, in approximately the same manner, Havel tartly replied, "Sure, sure. We anarchists make decisions. But we don't abide by them."

I brightened like a button on a flaring crimson rose.

I was soon delighted to discover that the majority of anecdotes about this drunken, wild-haired maverick feature him, minimally, mumbling if not actually shrieking, often on Greenwich Village street corners, "Goddamn bourgeois pigs!" (a past favorite epithet of my own). At Mabel Dodge's legendary salons at 23 Fifth Avenue, a "walrus-mustached, glittereyed" Hippolyte would wander, muttering among more than one hundred guests: modernist artists, writers, intellectuals and political activists of many stripes—their glorious and immemorial intermingling the ultimate cachet of that era for me. Self-described as a "species of head-hunter," some of Dodge's gatherings had mouth-watering themes.

Dangerous Character evenings alternated with Sex Antagonism, Family Planning and evening of Art and Unrest; she also held the first peyote party in the Village. Her salons must have been buzzing after the 1913 Armory Show which introduced New York to a host of sensational Cubist, post-Impressionist and Fauve paintings. Duchamp's "Nude Descending a Staircase" was the exhibit's *succes de scandale*—Duchamp himself arrived in New York two years later where he started creating his "readymades." (Contrary to the long-established assumption that all realists of John Sloan's generation were threatened by the Armory show, his biographer, John Loughery, claimed that many, including Sloan, realized the profound significance of the work.) At the end of an evening, Hippolyte would embrace Mabel with tears in his eyes. "My little sister! My little goddamn bourgeois capitalist sister!"

"It was the bloodiest day since the president became clinically insane."

Having often seen Hippolyte Havel mentioned in readings, I went to my *Anarchist Voices,* an oral history of anarchism in America, to find an array of his peers' accounts, and was excited to discover Sam Dolgoff's. Dolgoff, I knew, had traveled around the country, riding the rails, soap-boxing and organizing for the IWW, and I had just read his judicious introduction to a book of Bakunin's theoretical writings which pointed out Bakunin's ideological weakness: clinging to building a secret vanguard party (though *everything* had to be secret then) undermined many of the anarchists' most significant ideas about sharing power among federations of trade unionists and independent, organically formulated associations. But Dolgoff doggedly differentiated this transitional secret party from the Marxists' authoritarian central committee—his would explode. Bakunin must be judged on the whole of his thinking, Dolgoff insisted, which had so influenced 3rd world revolutionaries like Regis Debray and Frantz Fanon: emphasizing that the true revolutionary class consisted of lumpen-proletariat, the wretched of the earth, poorest and most disenfranchised rural workers, demonstrably déclassé intellectuals—seemingly everyone except for Marx' beloved advanced industrial workers who had too much to lose. *And still do* (insofar as they still exist).

Dolgoff had clearly liked Hippolyte personally, "an able writer and a man of broad culture," except he was quick to state that "he wrote mediocre pamphlets which contributed nothing to an anarchist theory." Describing the foppish Havel: "He was of medium height, with long hair, a thick mous-tache, spade beard, pince-nez, spats, cane, black ribbon tie, and narrow, tight-fitting trousers. He was witty and used colorful language enlivened by drink." Havel had a Czech accent, was a bon-vivant who went on frequent drunken sprees in the Village, looking "like a drowned muskrat" on his return. Other contemporaries in this volume viewed volatile Havel as resembling the caricature of the wild-eyed, bomb-throwing anarchist yet fastidious in his dress: a more or less delightful and irascible fellow, always right in the thick of things—but words like acrimonious, morose sponger, suicidal, and wasted talent also appeared not infrequently.

Absolutely everybody had anecdotes about his alcoholism. Once when Havel was brought before a judge and fined $5 for urinating in the streets—"You mean I don't even have the rights of a goddamn horse?" he raved to the policeman—he protested that the United States was the only civilized country without public comfort stations. He used to hang around the Brevoort Hotel to cadge free drinks. Another time after Havel had been ejected by the bartender and climbed back in through a window, an editor named Tom Smith bought him a few drinks and gave Havel his calling card. Havel got drunk, went outside, and sat, dazed, on a stoop. A cop saw him and brought him to Smith's house where Havel curled up on the rug and fell asleep. At the upstate New York, Mohegan commune, where Hippolyte briefly lived and waited on tables, health fads were the vogue. Asking what they drank, he was told water with a little milk. "'What's that?' said Hippolyte in horror."

As I read further, especially in Ross Wetzsteon's valuable *Republic of Dreams*, it became evident that for many in his day, Hippolyte Havel epitomized the very spirit of the Village, and of the "American Bohemian." To the delight of the intellectuals, Havel actually *came from* Bohemia and was the son of a Gypsy! One writer described him as "a legendary anarchist best remembered for declaring Greenwich Village a 'spiritual state of mind.'" (Nevertheless, they were lucky Village rents were so cheap—that changed in the '20s.) Several contemporary accounts of Havel's invention, the Trimordeur evening, describe wild dancing in the streets, and consider it one of the first occasions that Villagers began to develop a consciousness of their own Bohemian community. To evoke the Trimordeurs, knights-errant of the spirit of wine and dance, Havel had drawn up an invitation announcing a meeting at an Italian restaurant on Mulberry Street, and mailed postcards to ten or fifteen friends. On the night of the party, friends brought friends and friends of friends, and by midnight over 70 people were cavorting in the streets.

It was also evident that my fastening on Havel was a circuitous way of allowing myself to safely feel something other than despondency. Nostalgia, for starters—for Dionysian Bohemianism, which scarcely seems to exist anymore (thankfully, eccentricity definitely prevails among my friends), mostly due to our advancing years and to gentrification. Nostalgia for New York? I hadn't even been able to afford to visit in about 6 years, and had never really lived there—an effective way to maintain nostalgia—though I grew up ten miles north of the city in Yonkers, and spent chunks of months in Manhattan every year, mid-20s through mid-30s, including one semester of teaching. But it was clear if I'd stayed and taken the job the School of Visual Arts offered me, I would have lived in relative squalor in the east Village like everyone else. Decided against it, in fact, when I was contemplating the offer in Kathy Acker's 5th Street apartment, and suddenly heard her shrieking from the back (other) room—the ceiling had just fallen in on her! At least I wasn't indulging in regret, having adamantly never believed in it: you pays your penny and you takes your choice. Besides, when I returned to San Diego, I immersed myself in arts production and in grassroots politics again, making several close friends, and creating a much more defined niche for myself.

Not that youth was so great either, however Bohemian: if it had been, maybe nostalgia would be superfluous. Lots of sex in the pre-AIDS days—the best part by far, along with acid, and being somewhat bicoastal. But I was depressed and boyfriend-hunting much of the time; certainly no security in various part-time teaching jobs, mainly comp classes, which increasingly became a major burn-out till I refused to do them; health insurance wasn't even on the horizon till I was over 40. Middle age didn't offer much greater stability, and I felt its lack more keenly. Eventually, I wormed my way into getting coverage on a precarious, year-by-year basis for me and domestic partner, Joe. Then recently, out of the blue, I was told I'd have to pay for my own health benefits one quarter per academic year. So, in the months when I was only teaching one class, and my paycheck was already halved—not even enough to cover rent—most of it would go toward paying both our own *and* the university's share of those costs. I urged the statewide union people to "dialog" with the administration about their dastardly, new "interpretation" of the contract, and they did manage to get that decision reversed.

Coming on top of the union's winning a year-and-a-half long collective grievance in which UCSD employed every mean-spirited, nitpicking stalling tactic in the management handbook to keep from honoring the contract they'd signed, now for the first time at age 58, after almost 30 years, I was more or less guaranteed job and benefit security (and a modest salary) as a more-than-half-time, "continuing appointment" lecturer. Lucky that my new therapist had been so good at helping me deal with anxiety—*why* had it taken 30 years to get back into therapy? Actually, one reason the administration settled that grievance without going to arbitration, beyond the fact that they would have lost since they were in clear violation of the language they'd agreed to: they were desperate to get rid of the union rep, Sarah (I was her eager co-conspirator). Urging lecturers to file grievances, she was on top of every deadline, and when the administration invariably failed to provide access to information, she'd immediately file an unfair labor practice with the state. Then they'd give her wrong or inadequate information, and she'd file another.

No wonder it was easy to romanticize the past: my own situation was obviously much less dire; *I* didn't have to experience the shit that Havel and friends endured. From this distance, the hardships of being marginal back then tended to glamorize Havel, as it had apparently done for some of his contemporaries: maybe in part because he was such an insider, quite close to several key figures. In between excited political discussions, he served as cook in John Reed's (played by Warren Beatty in *Reds*) household in Provincetown. Frequently dismissed by Hippolyte as a parlor socialist, Reed rejoined with "kitchen anarchist!" ("The trouble with Havel," one of his crowd said, "is that he never gives *you* a chance to talk.") Havel loved the theater, acted in the Provincetown Players' productions both there and in New York (which attracted idiosyncratic talents like Djuna Barnes and Hart Crane), and regularly sponged off his friend, Eugene O'Neill, who based the character Hugo Kalmar in *The Iceman Cometh* on him, still muttering "bourgeois pigs." (I must read it!) Theodore Dreiser, who assiduously avoided Mabel Dodge's salons but hung out at the 8th Street bookstore, and the Holladays' restaurant, said, "Hippolyte Havel is one of those men who ought to be supported by the community. He is a valuable person for life, but can't take care of himself." Dreiser's vow to support him if he ever had any money may have been heartfelt but turned out to be meaningless.

Doubtless, Havel's symbolic import went beyond simple appreciation for his proto-Dada antics: he had truly suffered so much persecution. Yet another battered European political exile seeking intellectual freedom here. Finding it only briefly, of course, until the war tragically shut down dissent—censoring, incarcerating and deporting thousands, including Emma Goldman who had brought Hippolyte to New York as her lover (where he surfaced like a "ragged chrysanthemum," in Max Eastman's words) after they'd first met in London. (His hands were a mass of blisters then, so raw from hard physical labor that he wore gloves all the time which Goldman mistook for another sign of Havel's fastidious dandyism.) There, she wrote that he was a "veritable encyclopedia" who knew everything about the European movements. He had already been expelled from Vienna and Paris, tramped through Germany lecturing and writing, going to Zurich and, finally, London. Rather depressive and tongue-tied, Havel had come into the anarchist movement when he was 18 and had been in prison several times, once for 18 months. In the last, he was sent to the psychopathic ward where he might have remained indefinitely had he not aroused the interest of Professor Krafft-Ebbing who declared Havel eminently sane, and helped him to get released.

Certainly, Havel lived and worked at the very epicenter of Village activity. For awhile, he had a room at the Hermitage on 15th Street, where John Reed, Edna St. Vincent Millay and many others also lived. One interviewee in *Anarchist Voices*, going to visit Reed there, had smelled gas. Reed, who was a big man, ran up the stairs and broke down Havel's door. When they opened the windows, he came to. Havel basically fed the entire community, working as chef and waiter at the popular restaurant which Polly Holladay and her husband owned on MacDougal Street, directly beneath the political hub, the Liberty Club; he also worked at her Provincetown restaurant.

Polly was Havel's mistress; their relationship ran to extremes even for Villagers used to stormy love affairs. When he wasn't too drunk, Havel would affectionately greet her, "Hello, little monkey face." Once when a writer tried to hold him back from choking Polly, her brother remarked, "in a tone of restrained disgust, 'Don't you know they like it?'" (Her brother had once told Eugene O'Neill that Polly seduced him in early youth.) Still, Polly complained bitterly to a friend that Havel simply refused to commit suicide. "He promised me over and over again," she said earnestly, "but he just won't keep his word."

Havel lived in the basement of the Ferrer Modern School (some considered him a "mainstay"), part of a worldwide movement for libertarian education, and published the magazine *Revolt* there: prior to that, he had edited *Revolutionary Almanac*, funded by a wealthy Greek anarchist, a lover of Margaret Sanger who started Rabelais Press which published her sex hygiene articles in book form *(What Every Mother Should Know* and *What Every Girl Should Know)*. Ferrer schools were a response to Spain's mock trial and assassination of a radical educator (indicted for "having organized godless schools and godless literature") and were viewed by its enthusiasts as a model of what life could be without the usual organizational constraints. The director of its Free Theater remembers the Center as "a seething ocean of thought and activity, everybody working and creating," which offered both a children's school and adult classes in the arts, literature, physiology, psychology, Spanish, French and Esperanto. The day school was supervised by Will Durant (who married his 15-year-old student, Ariel Kaufman); evening art classes were taught by an impressive roster including Robert Henri, George Bellows and Man Ray; frequent speakers included Clarence Darrow, Margaret Sanger, Elizabeth Gurley Flynn, and Mike Gold.

Why did these names feel like such a grand litany to me? Admittedly, my tendency had always been to escape into the past, preferably into black and white movies, or else ensconced in a juicy 19th century novel, like *Middlemarch* (the longer the better). But an iconic, larger-than-life Wobblie like "Big Bill" Hayward, a longstanding personal favorite, interacting with modern artists like Stieglitz remains so impressive, impossible to picture at any other time; Wobblies themselves seem impossible at any time except when working conditions were utterly dire. Which they always are, of course, more or less—I guess today's perpetual barrage of a small number of ubiquitous media sound bites somehow mitigates against out-and-out class warfare!

About idealizing these particular icons from the past, my friend SPM posed the very reasonable question: why do I imagine them as less egotistical or pretentious than the New York art world I used to know? Plenty of interesting characters there; many huge egos and petty squabbles, enticing because they made you feel like an insider. (My friend Fanny Howe calls gossip "vitamin G.") Certain past luminaries, such as Emma Goldman, were well known to be intensely disliked; she and Margaret Sanger, chief birth control advocates, detested each other. But as Sanger deliberately moved away from her socialist past and into the mainstream, she remained close to communist organizers like Elizabeth Gurley Flynn, and Agnes Smedley. Many of the men were alcoholics—couldn't have all been the fun kind! Marsden Hartley had a brief infatuation with Nazism early on; Man Ray was supposedly a heavy-duty sadist. And once the First World War started, and a few leftists like Max Eastman supported it, the in-fighting must have been urgent, drastic, bitter.

Admirably, anarchists could organize effectively: they didn't all need chaos to thrive. The Ferrer Center lasted for 40 years. But not in Manhattan, where it quickly developed a reputation as a bomb factory, as a result of the infamous Ludlow massacre in Colorado. In April, 1914, during a coal miners' strike, a detachment of militia attacked a tent colony, killing five miners and a boy, then poured oil on the tents and set them ablaze: eleven children and two women were smothered to death. Following this, three people, including a strike leader, were savagely beaten and murdered. Amidst national protests, anarchists in New York hatched a scheme to blow up John D. Rockefeller's, the principal owner's, mansion near Tarrytown, New York. Alexander Berkman, Emma Goldman's lover who was later sent to prison for unsuccessfully attempting to assassinate Henry Frick, masterminded the plan at the Ferrer Center. On July 4, 1914, an explosion occurred in a nearby tenement on Lexington Avenue, killing three anarchists: the bomb had gone off prematurely. The Center lost most of its funding, was infiltrated with spies, and in its 4th year moved to Stelton, New Jersey for the remainder of its existence.

It was at Stelton in 1924 that Sam Dolgoff knew Hippolyte: he was editing *The Road to Freedom* (the publication continued till 1932), the first major periodical to appear since *Mother Earth* (founded in 1906) was suppressed when "Red Emma" was jailed in 1917; two years later, she was put on military transport and deported to Russia. Well past the heyday of U.S. anarchism, Abe Bluestein, another Stelton resident, reported that Havel was already "a superannuated figure" with no active role in the colony, "but wonderful to talk to." Oddly, "when drunk he made anti-Semitic remarks despite the fact that he was supported by Jewish friends all those years." In a 1910 monograph on Emma Goldman, Havel had praised her conservative parents for "receiving their sick daughter with open arms" when she was destitute, stating that "among the leading traits of the Jewish race is the strong attachment between parents and children." He went on to mention the "tremendous debt" in the realms of science, art, literature, and the revolutionary movement which the culture owed to Jews, "the race of transcendent idealism." Abe Bluestein finished his account of Havel: "This was the last phase of his life, and he was a declining man. Many were moved by pity for him at this point."

Next, the index of the oral history volume led me right to a brief yet mind-blowing passage from Nellie Dick who had started a Ferrer Center in London before visiting Stelton: "Hippolyte Havel made his best speeches while drunk. He was very irascible, very short with people. He ended his days raving mad in Marlboro State Hospital in New Jersey."

In my youth, I liked to believe that as long as I was sufficiently obsessed, nothing could touch me.

These were his declining tears and many were moved by pity for him.

11

That night I dreamt about Steven and Helen W., very close married friends from high school who I hadn't seen in decades: I was at some sort of high school reunion on a patio vaguely talking to a few people. Steven and Helen walked in. They were even shorter than I remembered; he was dressed in a pin- striped suit; they looked well tailored and miserable. I was so happy to see them, threw my arms around them both, started walking with Steven outside in a large, open grassy area that went way up a hillside, trying earnestly to explain that whatever Steven had done, he was innocent in my book. Then I suddenly remembered that I'd seen another Steven and Helen come into the party; I became confused, agitated, thought they were somewhere else, urgently needed to go find Steven and express my sympathy.

In truth, they *had* been on my mind a lot lately, since my mother sent me a front page *New York Times* article with a photo of them both outside the courthouse where Steven pled guilty to charges of corporate fraud. (I was wanting to contact them, but what could I say?—caught your pix in the *Times* today?) As chief counsel to a mega-corporation, he had instructed the lawyers beneath him to lie to federal investigators about inflated prof-its. Steven had turned state's evidence against the CEO and was evidently working out a deal. The article said he was facing a possible 25 years in prison and a $250,000 fine.

These old friends were *not* greedy bourgeois pigs, I just knew that; they did not fit any image I'd ever had of corporate profiteers. In high school, they had been part of our close-knit clique—we all saved each other's lives. They were sweet, studious, subdued, sardonic, not particularly materialistic. Steven's father was a cab driver, his mother an elementary school teacher: barely middle class. He started school at George Washington, worked hard to get a big scholarship to transfer to Ann Arbor. Helen's parents had more money, but she was deeply estranged from her father. In college, she'd been a Russian studies major; in high school, incongruously, a "brain" cheer-leader. The three of us were inseparable the summer after freshman year of college: together every single day after work, at my parents' house because they were away, we'd make dinner, hang out. Abruptly, after years of friendship, they fell madly in love near graduation, and absolutely yearned to be together. They got married that summer, and Helen left Boston for Ann Arbor where Steven was about to start law school.

I could envision their trajectory. Steven's expertise, steadiness, sharp wit, low-keyed and non- egotistical manner must have brought him better jobs and higher pay than he'd ever anticipated: his first job was in Dallas, doubtless they were thrilled to get back to New York. Moving to suburban houses much bigger than the ones they grew up in, their kids could go to expensive private schools and colleges; their lifestyle and debt level became firmly established. (About a year earlier, I had GOOGLED them and discovered both were philanthropically involved with Long Island arts agencies.) As chief counsel, Steven would have unequivocally been put into the position of aiding and abetting fraud or losing his job: there was no third option.

So they must have found themselves in a dark forest not knowing when they had entered: adjacent to my own, theirs familiarly marked beware-of-what-you-wish-for. Mine a more populous region: unfulfilled expectations, unappreciated "contributions"—in my case, experimental books completed and not published; students turned on by younger, flashy teachers; solipsistic, aggressive and trendy colleagues rewarded for just those disquieting qualities; my former years of activism seemingly to no avail. As we veer toward age 60, presumably we all, *all,* find ourselves in some common global thickets: deep fears about one's own health and that of friends and family; the palpable, resounding absence of many cherished dead. *(Today was the bloodiest day in the war since yesterday.)*

When I awoke from my Steven and Helen dream, I went on-line to try to find out more about Hippolyte's death. Till then, I'd been using my own fairly large library, collected partly due to phobia of the university libraries: in the past, I had invariably bumped into exactly the person there whom I most wanted to avoid (though, admittedly, that category bordered on the immense). For me the question was: HOW COULD I HAVE ALREADY READ SO MANY ACCOUNTS AND ANECDOTES ABOUT HAVEL AND NOTHING ABOUT INSANITY OR HIS

DEATH HAD COME UP? Had he been abandoned by friends and community?—dying alone and forgotten? Was he really "mad," or did they have no place else to stick him?

After several hours of GOOGLE, it became evident that a scholar (which I'm not) would pursue this in special collections at Rutgers and Ann Arbor. While Havel's hospital death was confirmed, I only learned that 1950 was the date (birth, 1871). Had he been living at Stelton all that time? Friends mostly predeceased him? I did discover a few random facts: colonists at Stelton had built a special room within their library for Havel to live and work. Recently, Bob Helms of the Wooden Shoe Collective in Philadelphia was trying to liberate Havel's ashes from a storage vault in Linden, New Jersey. I also read that the photographer Berenice Abbot had moved to MacDougal Street as a young woman, acted in O'Neill's plays, and was adopted as the "daughter" of Hippolyte Havel; he may have helped nurse her through influenza. (Like many Villagers, she had moved to Paris, way before Havel's final years.)

Skimming through various texts reminded me again how much I didn't know about the politics and history of this period. I came across some fascinating discussions of the assassination of President McKinley in 1901 by the self-proclaimed anarchist, Leon Czolgosz, who publicly declared that Emma Goldman had influenced him, while she countered that they'd never met: he belonged to no anarchist group and was generally thought to be deranged. Without one shred of evidence, the authorities attempted to establish Emma's complicity. They arrested Havel and other friends in Chicago, holding them with no charges, for ransom really, until Goldman turned herself in. Notoriously, Emma continued to defend Czolgosz's act through her trial and following her acquittal, incurring the ideological displeasure of some fellow anarchists as well as the wrath of the authorities and the media which dubbed her the most dangerous woman in America. For awhile, new mob attacks on anarchists erupted along with further state and federal anti-anarchy laws that remained rarely enforced until the war.

These laws, great-granddaddy to, and entirely consistent with, our own vile Patriot Act, aimed mainly at excluding immigrants, initially resulted from the infamous Haymarket affair in 1871: although often considered the beginning of anarchy's decline in the U.S., it did radicalize Emma Goldman, and many of the Wobblies. During a rally of locked-out strikers who were agitating for an eight-hour workday at McCormick Harvester, strikebreakers poured out of the plant; a battle ensued during which a bomb was exploded in the area held by the police, killing seven of them and four civilians. The bomber was never found. Ten leading anarchists were rounded up, and imprisoned after bogus trials; four were hanged. (Six years later, a new governor of Illinois commissioned a full inquiry, and the three remaining prisoners were released.)

Interestingly, Eva Brandes, a child of two anarchists, was only 3 at the time of the McKinley assassination but she remembers hearing that Czolgosz went to see Goldman in Chicago; wary of his talk of bombs and violence, she pretended to be someone else. When Eva was a little girl, she was sent into the jail where Chicago anarchists had been rounded up with Goldman, and she ladled out water for them from a bucket held by her mother. Brandes' vivid account of a lifetime involvement with talented, eccentric, multi-nationals in the stimulating Ferrer schools of New York and Stelton, at first sounded enticing. However, it ended with "a reign of terror" at the Mohegan colony where she was living after WWII. Paul Robeson was coming there to sing which brought a gang of Communist goons from the city patrolling the community with clubs and baseball bats, greatly harassing the residents; meanwhile the KKK, having previously burned a cross there, arrived in cars looking for the Communists. After the Peekskill riot in '49, the anarchists formed a civic association to isolate themselves from the Communists, but the colony was never the same.

How intriguing, those stories of repression, and particularly of partisan battles, factionalization, the left crippling itself—the familiar fascination with tearing at one's own wounds. Had I been kidding myself all along that the spirit of hope and expansive possibilities had chiefly attracted me to Havel's era? I had no doubts, though, concerning the magnetic confluence of avant-garde artists and politicos, maybe because in my own past, these people had formed rather distinct worlds. I *was* aware of, and admittedly titillated by, at least the contours of theoretical debates, and internecine battles among varied strands of anarchists, socialists, Marxist-Leninists, and labor leaders at the time, lasting through decades, and (thankfully) in a much vitiated form into the "New Left."

Also, in a startling revelation sometime in the late '80s, I had first learned of the inevitable, treacherous undertow in periods of progress, mostly visible later. At a party with several exceptionally bright students whose parents were then about my age, the conversation turned to the '60s, an era that I expected them to be idealizing. Instead, *all* their tales were chaotic and tragic: one student had been raised in a religious cult in LA; another related that when he was six, his mother committed suicide by jumping off the Golden Gate Bridge, presumably due to a bad acid trip. I appeared to be the only one to register surprise at his matter-of-fact tone or even at the story itself.

Was Hippolyte's awful ending gratifying my fatalism? (Looking for confirmation that nothing can improve seems so superfluous.) After all, though imperialism has always spelled evil, I had never trusted utopian thinking either: especially in Marxism where it elides right into dialectical materialism and "scientific" history with its absurd conclusion of an inevitable classless society. More charming in anarchism because it seems so fanciful and unsystematized: once upon a time, the world wasn't (or won't continue to be) filled with greedy human monsters.... Actually, if I had simply stopped to think, it shouldn't have been hard to predict the worst: a poor and visible, foreign-born anarchist who'd already essentially been tortured, living marginally in a country veering toward a catastrophic world war, with an intelligentsia badly demoralized, viciously repressed and splintered in its attempts to respond. Hippolyte Havel: ripe for the pickin'.

It began to feel like my library was a giant Tarot deck, with death and insanity being revealed at every turn. *(It was the bloodiest day since the president recently shot skeet.)* In Louis Shaeffer's biography of Eugene O'Neill, I came across the compellingly grim death of Louis Holladay (Polly's brother). O'Neill, Dorothy Day, when she was a writer prior to her heroic career founding the Catholic Workers, the painter Charles Demuth and several others were together one night at a friend's apartment. Holladay was depressed over a failed romance, and had obtained a bottle of heroin, probably from a shifty character at the Hell Hole, a seedy underworld bar that O'Neill, John Sloan and others of their crew frequented. Louis showed his friends the bottle; O'Neill declared that he was being reckless and rushed off into the night. (Some accounts say that Demuth also used the drug.) Not long afterwards, Holladay slumped over on Dorothy's shoulder, dead. Within seconds, she and the woman whose apartment it was were the only ones left in the room with the corpse. A policeman arrived, but Dorothy managed to take the bottle from Louis' pocket and hide it. Polly showed up, asserting to the coroner that her brother had heart trouble: the death certificate read chronic endocarditic condition.

Looking up the Holladays in that index, I then discovered their sister, Louise, had died by jumping off a steamer into the Hudson River (echoes of Hart Crane's oceanic leap). And Polly herself spent the final fifteen years or so of her life in a mental institution on Ward's island. GOD! Was that simultaneous with Havel's institutionalization? What would have happened if they'd wound up in the same place? Now assiduously hunting down disasters, back in the oral history text I read about Alexander Berkman's suicide—at least his ostensible reason was chronic physical pain. Deported to Russia with Emma Goldman, they left there to write separate books about disillusionment with the Bolshevik government (Goldman was horrified that hers was entitled such by her publisher). Berkman had taken up residence in Nice, earning a precarious living translating, editing and ghost-writing while being under constant threat of expulsion by the French government. In 1936, he underwent two operations for a painful prostate condition. Finally, in June of that year, he shot himself to death in his Nice apartment. (Just 3 weeks later the Spanish Revolution broke out, which Emma Goldman suggested might have revived his spirits.)

I'd seen too many friends die—in awesome and sacred mixtures of paranoia, rage, denial, stoicism, grace, and beatitude—to make any moral judgments or simple correlations about one's death and the quality of that person's life or work. Still, the idea of the energy and idealism of the pre-war period coming to naught was too depressing to sustain (even knowing how ruthlessly world leaders had built up to the First World War): I tried to think of exemplary figures whose accomplishments were enduring. Venerable Dorothy Day, speaking of transcendental idealism, and Margaret Sanger immediately sprang to mind: both were long-lived(!), having major impacts. And many of the artists and writers, whatever their personality quirks, did leave outstanding bodies of work. Additionally, collaborative efforts at creating alternative centers like Ferrer schools, and particularly media like *The Masses,* which didn't cater to any one cultural or political line exclusively, seem so crucial at all times.

Not that I judge people wholly by their accomplishments—more on what they care about, where they focus their energies, the quality of their compassion (of course, humor is invaluable). Makes me wonder how I'd feel about Steven and Helen now. Thinking back, one painful reason I was gradually estranged from them after college is that neither had become active in civil rights or during the Vietnam War. Without ever losing affection, they were increasingly remote from my own then obsessive need to act out rebellion, even before finally "coming out" in grad school. Recently, I GOOGLED Steven again to see if he'd been sentenced yet, and found several articles about his original testimony. I hadn't realized he was formerly a federal prosecutor. He was quoted as saying, "Your honor, I am ashamed to be standing here today," calling his actions "entirely inconsistent with my behavior during my 30-year legal career." I believed him: it made the dominant materialism (who can resist it? who doesn't yearn to be free of credit card debt?) feel especially insidious.

I'd always been a sucker for the contemptuous, "épater le bourgeoisie" attitude of Dada and much of the historical avant-garde: not generally regarded by political types as an overly persuasive tactic! Certainly, Hippolyte Havel appeared to wholeheartedly promulgate the rebellious spirit of his age: our imperative heritage. So I was pleased to come across this excerpt from a piece Havel wrote for *Mother Earth* in 1908:

> That they may not be continually reminded of their crimes against the proletariat, the exploiters have exiled them into obscure alleys, barrack tenements. There poverty lives apart. It is not suffered to obtrude its misery upon the rich, to the possible detriment of their digestion. There it does not exist for the bourgeois. It is to him a strange land.

This spoke precisely to my abhorrence of the bourgeois need for safety, to antiseptically isolate themselves which, growing up in the suburbs, was all too prevalent. Yesterday, swing vote Sandra Day O'Connor announced her retirement from the Supreme Court, most likely heralding the true beginning of the end for abortion rights and basic civil liberties, or perhaps announcing the staunch middle period of our decline—after all, hadn't the governor of Texas recently suggested that gays might choose to move to another state if they wanted any protection under the law. Not much room for optimism, but personally I had to admit I was feeling better.

I'd begun writing again, about Havel and the Wobblies, along the lines of previous pieces: historical anecdotes in a framework that was neither academic nor the simple, gimmicky fiction of a *Ragtime*. Until I stopped about two years ago, after seemingly futile, but ultimately successful, attempts to get my last book published, despite some excellent contacts in the ever-diminishing, small literary press world, I'd been writing steadily for over 30 years: maintaining the value of any art to be mainly that of unalienated labor. Writing was the one endeavor I did for its intrinsic rewards, to articulate something for my own well-being (and, secondarily, for any readers I might snare), to experience progress: basically, to keep from going nuts in a world way out of control. I had started *to feel that pleasure* again, viscerally, and now in a less compulsively workaholic way: what a tremendous relief. Also, I was keenly aware that my customary satisfaction in teaching had diminished considerably since I'd stopped writing: I seemed to be needing too much back from the students, then resenting them for not getting it. I fully expected that dynamic to be reversed next semester.

Naturally, my improving state of mind wasn't solely caused by the salutary spirit of melancholic yet acerbic Hippolyte Havel. But I felt he was a crucial catalyst, having found his brand of cosmopolitan anger inspiring, even reaffirming, particularly Havel's endearing incantation of "goddamn, bourgeois pigs." A durable, presumably heartfelt remonstrance against hypocrisy and solipsism, strongly resonating back to my own protest years, when my hair was long and unkempt, and I needed to be consistently confrontational: doubtless, to belie the underlying insecurities, also to believe I wasn't tacitly acquiescing to the system, even while realizing that opposition was its fundamental component. *("Today was the bloodiest day of the war since the president went on permanent vacation.")*

I really hoped my better mood wasn't due to contrasting my own choices and priorities to those of unfortunate old friends—not much compassion there! Needless to say, the summer was proving enormously beneficial for writing now that I was in that frame of mind, and for reading that's not all instrumental, i.e. directly useful for teaching. Also more time for friends. Therapy was undoubtedly key. Lucky to have found her (via my trusted doctor), especially in this town, where there are only two known good shrinks, both women, whom everybody sees (a little like the incestuous psych counseling center in college).

She seemed highly skilled at helping me feel less overwhelmed by, and indulgent in, my own spiraling arcs of anxiety, to view them as patterns of behavior which I could modify: originating in early wounds that, theoretically anyway, might be diminished by re-experiencing pieces of them. For instance, I could deal strategically with job issues, at which I've usually been fairly adept, while also trying to feel the original, classic double-bind (actually not so original—see Kafka!). To succeed in the world was to compete with/become like my materialist father and wholly mercantile family, thus negating my own "artsy" personality, as my parents had appeared quite eager for me to do in the past (current relations were quite satisfactory). To not succeed suggested that I'd been wrong to assert that gay, egghead self all along, and correct in feeling guilty for having done so: punishment would be final and severe. (Wonder if Hippolyte ever felt that kind of guilt. I'd be glad to believe not, and that his madness had more to do with impotent rage, in a world which had been inoculated against it by a horrific world war. But that's probably the most romanticized of all my projections onto him.)

So an attenuated mid-life crisis finally averted? Enjoying the scenery; unsure what's beyond the woods—except for more woods, obviously. Contemplation? Intuition? The creation of angels?

111

I meant to read *The Iceman Cometh,* but had already started the much-anticipated *War and Peace,* and still had John Sloan's saga to complete: in 1925, he'd gotten involved with the *New Masses* and was rapidly becoming disenchanted with its CP line. Also with several mss. which colleagues had asked me to read, I felt anxious that the summer was slipping away. So I skimmed *Iceman* instead, looking for all the places where Hugo Kalmar, the Havel character, spoke. These were few, since Hugo is passed out through the entire play, only sporadically awakening to deliver drunken mono-logs. (The action takes place in a bar over a 2-day period.) Hugo Kalmar is described like Hippolyte: a head too big for his body, nearsighted behind thick-lensed spectacles, "crinkly long black hair streaked with gray," walrus mustache, threadbare but fastidiously dressed ("even his flowing Windsor tie is neatly tied"). He has "the stamp of an alien radical, a strong resem-blance to the type Anarchist as portrayed, bomb in hand, in newspaper cartoons."

The characterization is sad. Hugo's brief rants scan almost instanta-neously—sentimental, angry, deathly afraid:

> **Hugo** *(With his silly giggle)*: Hello, Harry, stupid proletarian monkey-face! I will trink champagne beneath the villow—*(With a change to aristocratic fastidiousness).* But the slaves must ice it properly! *(With guttural rage)* Goddamned Hickey! Peddler pimp for nouveau-riche capitalism! Vhen I lead the jackass mob to the sack of Babylon, I vill make them hang him to a lamppost the first one!
>
> Someone then offers Hugo a drink, and he suddenly becomes frightened: "Vhat's matter, Harry? You look funny. You look dead. Vhat's happened? I don't know you. Listen, I feel I am dying, too. Because I am so crazy trunk. It is very necessary I sleep. But I can't sleep here with you. You look dead."

Sounds suspiciously like the "superannuated" Hippolyte who Dolgoff knew at Stelton in 1924. But this play takes place in 1912. Could O'Neill have viewed him that way as a younger man? I prefer to believe not. Actu-ally, the Kalmar character is supposed to be in his late fifties, and in 1912, Hippolyte was about 40. O'Neill wrote the play in 1939, so it's likely he was interpolating a contemporaneous Havel into the past.

Perhaps O'Neill had seen Havel deteriorate, and that made a lasting impression. In my own experiences, it can take years after their death to really remember a person, *to see them*, in any way other than debilitated and failing. When my friend, the writer Sherley Anne Williams, was dying of cancer, we would joke on the phone like old times, but when I said I wanted to come visit, she replied, "please don't." After she died, I silently thanked her. The funeral had a closed casket, so my strongest memories of her are hanging out in our late 30s, early 40s: vital and lucid, she was unbelievably funny, especially about the way blacks were treated in the academy (simultaneously patronized and eroticized).

Then a genuinely creepy thought hit me. Of course, Havel was still alive when O'Neill wrote the play in '39—presumably in the mental hospital already, or careening right toward it. Maybe O'Neill didn't even know that. Did he care? (He'd won the Nobel Prize by then, and was probably on a distant star.) Did *anybody* care?

It was the bloodiest day in the war since yesterday, leetle monkey face.
Ah, Hippolyte! Ah, humanity!

Hippolyte Havel

SUPERMAN VS. ATOM MAN:
radio play

THE ATOM MAN-EPISODE L826

ANNOUNCER: Escaping to Germany with a piece of the stolen kryptonite fragment which robs Superman of his strength, Dr. Teufel, a brilliant Nazi scientist, made his way to a secret cave in the Black Forest where several leading Nazis were preparing the hides.

Teufel told Professor Milch, a chemist, that if the kryptonite could be dissolved, the resultant solution, injected into the veins of one of their followers, would create Atom Man—a human monster generating sufficient atomic energy to not only exterminate Superman but to bring the whole voracious and sad world deep into naked terror.

Dr. Teufel sent this human monster, a young German using the name Adam Miller, back to Metropolis where he was "educated" mainly in mixing metaphors in elbow grease. As his first assignment, he was to find and conquer Superman! Speaking almost perfect English, Miller secured a position as a reporter on the *Daily Planet*, and the blond Aryan wearing a leaded vest was introduced to a frankly unnerved Clark Kent.

In the presence of the kryptonite in Miller's blood, Kent became momentarily dazed and irrational: then that irrepressible gent, Kent, actually began eating cotton! Believing that he was losing his mind, Lois Lane had Kent taken for observation to a mental institution, from which The

Man of Steel escaped that evening. Returning to the seemingly deserted *Planet* office, he found Miller rifling Lois' drawers, and challenged him:

SUPERMAN (UP, FADE IN): Having a good time, my friend?

MILLER (OFF, WHEELING): Superman!

SUPERMAN (SLIGHTLY OFF): Is that all you've got to say?

MILLER (PAUSE): No! I'll have something more to say—in just a moment!… Let's see.… "'She cocked her ear and heard only the silence'—muttered the rancher thickly."

ANNOUNCER: Quickly, Miller's hands dart into his jacket pockets, fumbling for the metal mesh gloves and electronic throat-converter that will transform him into deadly Atom Man. And unaware of his great danger, Superman stands in the doorway, arms akimbo, disdainful smile playing upon luscious lips.

STUDIO: TWO PAIR QUICK STEPS—ONE HIGH HEELS COMING IN

JIMMY OLSEN (FAR OFF-APPROACHING): Gosh, I nearly walked into that loin stump.… But honest, Miss Lane, our anthro prof, Joachim C. Fest, claimed that it's no coincidence that for years no one has found his way into the top Nazi leadership who has a family or whose family life matches the image of national socialist ideology. In countless and tirelessly presented metaphors, pictures, monuments, as well as in the amateurish but officially fostered "genuinely national poetry," the type is pictured as a heroic figure, preferably on his own land, gazing boldly into the rising sun or standing with legs apart as he offers his strong bare chest to the turbulent waves of life. This erect blond idol with the unmistakable aura of male sweat and nobility of soul is particular to all stylizations of national socialist ideology, in whatever form.

LOIS LANE (WEARY): Leaning against him is his tall, full-bosomed wife: she is doughty and valiant, but at the same time fervent, profound and gay amid the children to whom she tirelessly gives birth. (SUDDEN ANGER) YOU KNOW THE REALITY IS THEY'RE FUCKIN'

BREEDING NAZIS RIGHT NOW, JIMMY BOY. By the mid-1930s centers were being set up to enable human stock breeding: SS men impregnate girls whose physical appearance qualifies them to come up with evidence of their Aryan blood traceable back to the Thirty Years War. Their parents, ancestors, ideals, loyalty, and devotion to the Fuhrer are also inquired into. Many are so fanaticized that they sign a declaration abjuring Christianity in favor of the new religion of blood. The SS children are to be the advanced guard of the race that is to populate the planet for a thousand years.

STUDIO: FOOTSTEPS, APPROACHING

PERRY WHITE: Poppycock!

JIMMY OLSEN (RUSTLING PAPER): Jumping Jemima, chief! Just *listen* to this marriage advertisement from a German newspaper:

> 52-year-old, pure Aryan physician
> fighter at Tannenberg, wishing to settle down,
> desires male offspring through civil marriage
> with young, healthy virgin of pure Aryan stock, undemanding
> suited to heavy work and thrifty,
> with flat heels, without earrings, if possible without money.
> No marriage brokers. Secrecy guaranteed.

LOIS LANE (PAUSE): Flat heels, huh? For fuck's sake!

JIMMY OLSEN: I wish all my classmates were live wires like that wino Nancy Drew!

PERRY WHITE: Good Godfrey! Nancy…is she…"blotto?"

STUDIO: DOOR OPENS—DRAWER SLAMS

MILLER (DIDACTIC): The woman who voluntarily renounces motherhood is a deserter! No foreign slave housemaids for her! *Pas de tutti-fruti! (CERTAINLY NO GERMAN MOTHER'S CROSS FOR THAT SLUT!)*

LOIS LANE: So *that's* why you're rifling through my drawers, Mr. Miller? Or is that a piston in your pantaloons?

MILLER (CASUAL): I can't explain, Miss Lane. (TITTERS) a little poem! I missed my gold cigarette case at dinner and I thought I might have left it in your ratty old drawers which are right next to my robust coat of arms. This is my first day at the *Planet*, you know, and I must've mistaken your office for my indifference to your plight.

JIMMY OLSEN (COUNTRY TWANG): Well, I'll be dinged!

PERRY WHITE and LOIS LANE (SIMULTANEOUS, DISDAINFUL): *We* know. Sometimes it feels like you et the larkspur.

SUPERMAN (THROUGH FILTER): Dang this strange weakness! It's the same as when you were in the presence of the kryptonite. Could Adam Miller be packing cotton?

LOIS: Are you ill again, Superman? WAIT!—"again?" That was *Clark Kent* who was ill.… (EXCITED) Superman! Are *you* pissing cotton?!

SUPERMAN (THROUGH FILTER): Wait! That ring on Lois' finger. Look at it! *A green stone.* Milky-green! Great scott! Perhaps it's—

LOIS: Here—drink water, Superman!

JIMMY OLSEN (PAUSE): Is he swallowing?

LOIS: Not yet. We ought to have a doctor—hey look! He's starting to swallow!

JIMMY OLSEN (TENTATIVE JOY): He is? I don't think he's coming yet!

LOIS (IRRITATED): What use is your dried up, egghead professor anyway, Jimmy? That old reprobate paid absolutely no attention to the *few* women in my class at State—except to slobber ridiculously all over poor Betty and Veronica. Why, he'd never even heard of Rosa Luxemburg! And he's surely not fit to kiss the hem of one fuckin' freedom fighter's foot (should she choose to wear one)!

PERRY WHITE (RISING APOPLEXY AS HE WALKS AWAY): GREAT SCOTT! The hem of a foot?!

JIMMY OLSEN: Say tenderfoot, you're plumb loco! Didn't Professor McCock tell us all about Gerda Bormann, wife of Martin Bormann, whose imperturbable attachment to the person of the Fuhrer went hand in hand with a simple, literal, ideological seriousness open to every intellectual claim, no matter how unreasonable. "Oh Daddy," she once wrote Bormann, "every word which the Fuhrer said in the years of our hardest struggles is going round and round in my head again.... Without knowing it, Luther wrote a real Nazi song! I'm worried about Charlemagne's responsibility for the introduction of Christianity and Jewry into Central Europe!"

LOIS LANE (MUTTERS): Good thing we didn't step in it!

JIMMY OLSEN: When Bormann told her about his successful seduction of the actress "M," Gerda suggested that he bring M home with him, and that they work out a system of shift motherhood and finally "put all the children together in the house on the lake, and live together, and the wife who is not having the child will always be able to come and stay with you in Obersalzberg or Berlin."

LOIS LANE: I know. (MIMICKING) "I'm only worried that you haven't given that poor girl a frightful shock with your imperious ways." Actually, Jimmy, that little ménage sounds a lot like Simone de Beauvoir and Sartre's cunning arrangements. Not to mention like my own juicy fantasies which I rarely even allow myself to indulge, featuring servile Clark Kent and studly Superman. No fascists, us! Of course, we have no children either. (PAUSE) Say, Jimmy, did you ever notice how Clark is never around when you want to fuck him?

JIMMY OLSEN: Don't you mean when you want *him* to want to fuck *you*, Miss Lois?

LOIS LANE: Anywhoo, the point is while the Germans are über-efficient death machines, we're all too complex for our own good. Except, of course, for simple Sally Superman—so where *is* that heavenly hunk? Seems to have whisked himself away (THOUGHTFUL)...*sans erectionne*, I wonder?

JIMMY OLSEN: DREAMY!

LOIS LANE: I bet your precious old McCock doesn't know that Bormann is currently conspiring with heinous Himmler so that German soldiers can have more than one wife, because women "cannot receive their children from the Holy Ghost, but only from those German men who are still left." The first wife would be titled "Domina," and more wives would be bestowed on holders of the German Cross in gold as well as the Knight's Cross: recently extended to holders of the Iron Cross as well as those holding the silver and gold close-combat bar. After all, doesn't "Herr" Hitler always say, "The greatest fighter is entitled to the most beautiful woman."

JIMMY OLSEN (INDIGNANT): Naturally, it's absolutely impossible for any Aryan broad to get an abortion nowadays while being totally mandatory for pregnant Jewish prisoners.

MILLER: Before leaving, I just want to say in my own defense that my teachers made me do it! They were all deeply anti-Semitic and Germanic high culture was clearly a reflection of their own vicious prejudices.

LOIS LANE: See, Olsen, I told you it's all the fault of those feshugenah professors! And even though I'm a career woman who respects intellect, I'm only half kidding!

JIMMY OLSEN: *That's* why we need Superman to not think for us!

MILLER: Hop my paw, little missy!

JIMMY OLSEN: *I* listen to you?

LOIS LANE: Nonsense! The Fascists and Nazis succeeded in large part because they echoed the voices and interests not of a handful of conservative intellectuals, but of aristocratic landowners, military leaders, reactionary industrialists, small shopkeepers, and small-holding peasantry.

MILLER: However, that is not to underestimate the fatal German concept of education which excluded politics, and made it the despised business of dubious characters or a matter for "strong men." It was an idea which compensated for lack of civil liberty by a retreat to "inner freedom" and cultivated both a misguided political abstinence and a political consciousness saturated with heroic concepts. It understood the state not as a system of checks and balances for the protection of individual liberties but as an absolute quantity with extensive claims to submission, as a sacred entity—

LOIS LANE (DRIPPING):—yeah, a hard cock.

MILLER: These and many other intellectual circumstances helped to create a long and wretched tradition of whole generations of university teachers, literary pseudo-prophets and presidents of nationalist societies in which hostility to reason, brutalization of life and corruption of ethical standards required only to be crystallized in a genocidal political outlook in order to—

LOIS LANE: Yaddah, yaddah! (GRANDLY) He who can't spell history is doomed to misspell it!

ANNOUNCER (AT WIT'S END): Atom Man slips into the dark woods and begins working his way toward the huge reservoir—poised like a giant spittoon above Metropolis. Can anyone—or anything—top him now(!), this man in whose very blood runs the deadly atomic energy of kryptonite? The Man of Steel faces his most desperate challenge in the next episode of THE ADVENTURES OF SUPERMAN!

THE ATOM MAN-EPISODE L830

ANNOUNCER: Using Jimmy Olsen as bait, Adam Miller, in whose veins flows deadly atomic energy, lured Superman to a lonely beach far from Metropolis with additional promises of far-reaching dudes. Wearing meshed metal gloves, Miller touched the switch at his throat; from his fingers purred a stream of terrible atomic power! After a titanic battle, Superman fell unconscious, and the Atom man, joined by Der Teufel, the half-mad fugitive Nazi scientist who plans to rule the world, prepared for tit-i-llation.

Meanwhile, escaping from the shack where he had been held prisoner, a slim-hipped yet horny Jimmy raced back through the lilac bushes in search of help—and as we continue now, he has come to a small queering, in which stands the rough hut of a randy rabbit-trapper. Pantingly, he pounds on the door:

STUDIO: POUNDING ON DOOR.

TOM (RABBITER) (MUFFLED): Take it easy. I'm a' comin'.

STUDIO: DOOR OPENS.

TOM: What's the rush, son?

JIMMY OLSEN (PANTING): Excuse me. I-I'm Jim Olsen.—Can I—use your phone?

TOM: I haven't got a phone out here. (CHUCKLES) Now, what would I do with a phone?

JIMMY OLSEN (GROAN): Oh golly, what'll I do? I'm about as welcome here as two snowballs in Hades!

ANNOUNCER: Hair standing on end, Jimmy Olsen wheels like a frightened deer and plunges back into the bush—his eyes wide with the horror of what he has seen. Onward, he races—tripping-falling—picking himself up and plunging on through the forest filled with that awesome rumbling. (PAUSE) Tom's tanned, rugged face takes on a look of deep concern.

TOM (SHOUTING): Now listen, young fellow, just try to calm yourself down. You're jittery and keyed up—like most of those city folk. You can send a message with my muffins—it'll give all those damn fidgety hands of yours something to do. (DIGNIFIED) So just get on the grub line, hombre, and shut your hole!

JIMMY OLSEN (INSULTED): *WELL!* I'm going to tell Superman!... Say, aren't you in my anthro class?

TOM: Yeah, he's got a big house and everything.

JIMMY OLSEN: Say, isn't your name Adam Smith? Or Henry Miller? (VAGUELY SUSPICIOUS) Or A-tom Bomb Man, something or other....

TOM: It's just plain Tom, dude, as in cat. Everyone knows that!

JIMMY OLSEN: Whatever, punster dude. You know, I *still* can't comprehend that banality of evil stuff—how Dr. Moorcock is always saying the Nazis are mainly bureaucrats. But whatever happened to *really* virulent, carefully orchestrated anti-Semitism like the good ol' Crusades or Spanish Inquisition? I presume you know that Doc M'cock predicts that scholarly inquiry will reveal "the predominant type lacked even unmitigated criminality; he had preserved the petty bourgeois attitudes and impulses of his origin; his fanaticism as expressed in unthinking efficiency. Pedantic, with a murderous 'love of his job,' he always did only what he conceived as his duty, and, like Himmler or Hesse, was completely incapable of understanding his terrible reputation."

TOM: Yeah, I know all about how much they love their dogs and all that shit.

JIMMY OLSEN (RECITING): "The daily practice of murder and almost tender family relationship, discussions of the technical improvement of the 'fuel capacity' of the incineration ovens and the almost legendary musical evenings by candlelight...."

TOM: Nothing wrong with *my* oars!

JIMMY OLSEN: Say, do you need a study partner, dude?

TOM (ROARING): How's about a fuck buddy, son?

JIMMY OLSEN (HASTILY): On January 7, 1932, Hitler's most famous speech was appealing to the elite of Germany's industrialists at Düsseldorf to expand the large sums they were contributing to his mounting campaign expenses. He assured the industrialists that rearmament on a vast scale would provide them markets, stop militant trade unionism, and end unemployment. Most important of all, perhaps, he told them that no matter what they might have heard, national socialism stood for the sacred property rights of private property. Only if these rights were honored, he insisted, could Germany gain the economic strength needed for a policy of iron determination abroad.

TOM: Too often scholars have stressed the ideological and political differences between old conservatives and new ultraconservatives but have failed to perceive how willing the respectable conservatives have been to trade these differences with their own ultra-rightwing in order to prevent the victory of liberalism and the triumph of mass education.

JIMMY OLSEN: For land's sake!

TOM: (Tough luck some hombres have: you're pale clear as a gill!) Come this way—to the cellar. Hurry. There is a tunnel under the floor—I will show you. It will take us under the edge of the forest—to the hidden cave on the beach with its pay phone (SLURPING), half-naked cabana boys, and quite a gaunt iguana. Now that's what *I* call one hell of a piece of *private property*.

JIMMY OLSEN: That's what I'm talkin' about!

TOM: Come on, we've got things to do! Big things.

ANNOUNCER: CYCLONE BLOWED OVER—SHINDIG UNDER WAY AGAIN! As Jimmy Olsen is getting rimmed, a few miles away on the beach, the Atom Man, nipples blazing like diamonds, stands by impatiently as Teufel bends over the limp, motionless figure of Superman. All about is a scene of chaos. Great trees ripped from the beach, branches of the sausage tree, split and blackened as if by lightning, lie all about in crazy smoked profusion; as usual, lots of luscious limbs akimbo.

The vast beach, from the gray sea to the edge of the forest, is gashed and torn into deep trenches and craters, almost as if it had sustained an artillery barrage. Finally, the Atom Man steps forward impatiently, again speaking in the "normal" voice of Adam Miller.

MILLER (FADING IN): Well, Teufel—are you satisfied that he's dead?

DER TEUFEL (COLDLY): He is *not* dead!

MILLER: He must be!

DER TEUFEL: I tell you he is not; his heart still beats. Very faintly, but it still beats.

MILLER: Impossible! That huge tree that lay across his legs—it's entirely denuded!

DER TEUFEL: But Superman still lives! (ANGER RISING) What must we do to kill him? *What?*

MILLER: I tell you he's dead. But if it'll make you feel any better, I'll turn on my converter again, and wipe that fuckin' commie fag off the fuckin' face of the fuckin'—

DER TEUFEL: Nein! You must not! The atomic energy in your blood can be exhausted. You have already consumed a great deal of it today, and you only have one more giant wad to shoot all over my exquisite face!

MILLER: But what if that *isn't* enough to make everyone in the world into a fetid mess of slobbering zombies, and I've exhausted the atomic power of the kryptonite?

DER TEUFEL (ABSENTLY): In that case, there is always the Scarlet Widow. She has the other three pieces of kryptonite luggage.

MILLER: She has? The leatherette towel holder too?

DER TEUFEL (ABSENTLY): Ja. She—(PAUSE) Ach!

ANNOUNCER: This is *not* the moment we've all been waiting for! Don't miss the next senselessly breathless, exciting episode of Superman in which the sanguinary Scarlet Widow, who dreams of big-time escape into the Argentine, along with several other silly stock characters, will most certainly (not) make an appearance: Sydney the fat man who shakes with greedy laughter, Jito his ruthless "Oriental" houseboy whose slyness is rewarded with chocolates, and a nameless German prisoner who has just been brought in, a squat, slack-jawed man who seems ill at ease in his handsome frock coat and silk hat. What tomorrow's episode *will* reveal, however, are reassuringly explosive titanic battles enacted all around that damn dam guarding the great billion dollar reservoir in the hills above the city—the first sparks of jagged green lightning which leaped from his weirdly glowing hands, plowing an enormous crater—faster and faster the pale moon lighting his billowing red cape and shimmering on the various silvery waters of the vast, vivacious spittoon.... (VOICE FADES TO DISGRUNTLED MUMBLING)

THE ATOM MAN EPISODE L836

ANNOUNCER: And now, manically, the great lightning leaps—ever lengthening—and is almost at the dam, when (BURST WIND AND SUSTAIN IT) Superman flashes upward from the deep waters of the reservoir, his costume and cake dripping, and rockets like a birthday bullet at the Atom Man! Later, his candles all blown out and left for dead on a lonely beach by Adam Miller, the Atom Man, Superman is brought to a country hospital, where he lays in a coma for many hours, his identity unknown. But the following morning, weak and dazed, he manages to make his way back to Lois Lane's chic flat, where he and Lois could only exchange strange words.

LOIS LANE (IMITATES BETTE DAVIS): What a dump. Hey, what's that from? "What a dump!"

SUPERMAN: *Who's Afraid of Virginia Woolf?!* How would I know what....

LOIS LANE: Aw, come on! WHAT'S IT FROM, FOR CHRIST'S SAKE?

SUPERMAN: I haven't the faintest idea what....

LOIS LANE: Dumbbell! It's from some goddamn Bette Davis picture.... Bette Davis gets peritonitis in the end...she's got this big black fright wig she wears all through the picture and she gets peritonitis, and she's married to Joseph Cornell or something....

SUPERMAN: ...Some*body*....

LOIS LANE: somebody...and she wants to go to Chicago all the time, 'cause she's in love with that sculptor with the scar....

SUPERMAN: *Chicago!* It's called *Chicago*.

LOIS LANE: Good grief! Don't you know *anything*? *Chicago* was a '30s musical, starring Miss Alice *Faye*. Don't you know *anything*?

SUPERMAN: Well, that was probably before *my* time....

STUDIO: TWO PAIR QUICK STEPS APPROACHING

TOM (FROM A DISTANCE): No emotion either carries Himmler away or inhibits him. His very coldness is a negative element, not glacial, but bloodless: a man at freezing point. Yet his character, almost abstract in its colorless impersonality, gains a certain individuality from his eccentric views. With naïve certainty, Himmler considers himself the reincarnation of Heinrich 1, who had done battle with the Hungarians and Slavs. He recommends a breakfast of leeks and mineral water for his SS, will only have 12 people as guests at his table, following the example of the Royal Table of King Arthur, and is occasionally to be found in the company of high SS officers all staring fixedly into space in an attempt to compel a person in the next room to confess the truth by their "exercises in concentration."

JIMMY OLSEN: At least Perry White isn't into *that*—it's more exercises in *per*spiration! Like yesterday, he was ranting (FURIOUS MIMICKING WHITE MIMICKING JIMMY) "'He said! He said! If you don't stop repeating that, I-I-I don't know what I'll do! (FADING) Now come on—both of you.'" (PAUSE) That reminds me. When we get to Lois', honey, *pleeeease* don't rant about Himmler. You *know* how she can get—like a small animal rustling around in a candy box.

STUDIO: DOORBELL CHIMES

LOIS LANE (SHOUTING): Darlings! George, get them a drink. (DOOR SQUEAKS OPEN) What's that picture where Bette Davis comes home from a hard day at the grocery store, and....

JIMMY OLSEN: She works in a grocery store?

LOIS LANE: No silly, she's a housewife, she buys things...and she comes home with the groceries, and she walks into the modest living room of the modest cottage modest Joseph Cotton has set up for her in....

JIMMY OLSEN: Are they married?

LOIS LANE: Yes. They're married. To each other. Cluck! And she comes in, and she looks around, and she puts her groceries down, and she says, "What a dump!"

TOM: Himmler's peasant superstitions, naturally, after the fashion of the time, have pseudo-scientific trimmings. He has archaeological excavations carried out in search of the original pure Aryan race and studies made of the skulls of "Jewish-Bolshevik commisars" in order to arrive at a typological definition of the "sub-human."

JIMMY OLSEN (STAGE WHISPER): Hon—*eee!*

LOIS LANE: Ha! I presume you know Hitler has begun negotiations for the resettlement of five million Dutch farmers in the conquered territories of the east. In the east, the Nazis neither expect nor want cooperation from the subject peoples. Poland and Russia are to have all vestiges of community life and national consciousness destroyed. Under the notorious Hans Frank, some of the policies have begun in Poland. Polish intellectuals, landlords, and political leaders are being slaughtered. Polish literature and even the language are to be obliterated. In Bohemia and Moravia, student leaders are shot, politically minded clergy exterminated, and the publication and study of Czech literature and history forbidden.

TOM: Only unskilled workers and peasant masses are to remain in the east—all higher tasks are to be reserved for the Nordics.

JIMMY OLSEN: See, Lois, that *proves* that intellectuals do have power.

LOIS LANE: You've got a valid point there, hon. But you've *got* to start drinking more and fantasizing less about Professor McCock! Didn't your analyst warn you?

JIMMY OLSEN (POINTEDLY): If H.G. Wells hadn't broken his leg, he might still be clerking in a dry goods store.

SUPERMAN: Well, Herr Himmler seems to agree with you about brain power, Jimmy. He has just proposed the "Women's Academies of Wisdom and Culture" for superior-type Aryan women who would be given "a good grounding in history," a knowledge of several languages, and—needless to say—special courses in cookery and housekeeping. The Exalted Woman's training would also include riding, swimming, car-driving, and pistol shooting.

LOIS LANE (DISGUST): Quel improvement! Hitler's previous highest accolade for women—the German Mother's Cross—was awarded on August 12, his mother's birthday. A bronze cross is awarded for four to six children, silver for six to eight, and gold for eight or more. When wearing their decorations these women are entitled to the Hitler Youth Salute as well as to all sorts of privileges and special slave shipments of Eastern Europe housemaids.

TOM (AGITATED): Jesus, even when Genghis Khan and the Mongol hordes conquered the world, they encouraged indigenous arts and crafts. Under them, Chinese theater flourished, Confucian and Tibetan Buddhist monks were employed, the construction of temples and monasteries encouraged. In Iran, the Mongol era witnessed an outpouring of great historical writings. Mongols funded medicine and astronomy throughout their domain, and promoted science and engineering. This included the extension of China's Grand Canal and the development of a sizable network of roads and postal stations.

STUDIO: FOOTSTEPS APPROACH, DOOR OPENS

JIMMY OLSEN: Chief!

PERRY WHITE: And how many times have I told you not to call me "chief," Olsen?

JIMMY OLSEN: Sorry, boss, sometimes I just like to slip it in.

SUPERMAN (PEREMPTORY): Perry! Let's have lots of drinks!

TOM (DEFIANTLY): For the so-called superior Aryan race, not even a Nazi Russian could be allowed to exist. As Erich Koch, the prime executor of this program put it, "If I find a Ukranian worthy of sitting at the same table with me, I must have him shot."

PERRY WHITE: Lighten up you big galoot, this is a shindig. I'd like to propose a toast to George and Martha's inauguration—long may they wave!

LOIS LANE: Here, here! To the mother and father of our beloved upper classes…er, I mean nation! (SARDONIC CHUCKLE) And to the progenitor of the mighty *Planet!* Hail to Chief Perry "Whitey" White!

JIMMY OLSEN: Über-mensches, über alles! (Oops! *What made me say that?*)

STUDIO: SOUND OF CLINKING, THEN SHATTERING, GLASSES AND CURSING

PERRY WHITE: Now, now! Martha! George! The first Continental Congress asked me to present you with this ceremonial pewter wig, and lovely imitation leatherette towel holder.

SUPERMAN: I get the joke, I've been to college like everybody else.

LOIS LANE: Martha been to college (MUMBLES) like all those rich men. *Un*like Thom Paine, the *only* one of those feshuggenah guys with any common sense: the only one who really cared about liberty, and not just protecting their precious property rights. Why—

SUPERMAN (CUTTING HER OFF): Martha been to a Marxist convent when she were a little twig of a thing too. You know, when I married Martha, she was one of the richest widows in Virginia. She came with 150,000 acres of land and about 150 slaves. Not that I needed her money—I was already a huge real estate speculator. And I also had tenure, and her father's money or his hands were in my pockets, or wherever….

LOIS LANE: And I was an atheist. (UNCERTAIN) I still am.

SUPERMAN: Not an atheist, Martha…a pagan. The only true pagan on the eastern seaboard.

PERRY WHITE: Tut, tut yourself…you old floozie!

JIMMY OLSEN: He's not a floozie...he can't be a floozie...you're a floozie. (GIGGLES) *What am I saying?*

PERRY WHITE: Need I remind you the *Planet* is an *open shop*, "mister" Olsen?

JIMMY OLSEN: I'd like a nipper of brandy, please.

TOM: I think you've had enough now....

JIMMY OLSEN: *I* listen to you?

ANNOUNCER: To the surprise of everyone, Bess totally comes speeding up the driveway in her cherry red roadster. They had assumed she was in the kitchen, sprawled out all over Miss Lois' bright yellow linoleum countertops. She and the other sparky teens enter the house and Bess jumps up and says excitedly, "I brought some meat with a tranquilizer in it." "You what?" George and Martha demand, tipsily. Bess explains that "he" could not come himself but had given her the chunk of raw meat with a tranquilizer pill imbedded in it like a reporter in a hawk. The others stare at her in amazement. Finally, Nancy Drew topples off the diva(n) where she'd been tippling mightily, and titters, "That's wonderful, Bess. It was 'stinkin' thinkin'."

JIMMY OLSEN (DIDACTIC): Cyclone blowed over—shindig under way again!

NANCY DREW (HEARTFELT): Thanks, Superman, for saving the world! You did a wonderful job. Simply wonderful. We've had a recent report of what would have happened at the reservoir if not for you. (SHIVER) Every man, woman, child, and floozie in Metropolis would have been dead by now.

JIMMY OLSEN: We owe you more than we can ever repay, *but we'd sure like to try.* (SLURP)

TOM & LOIS LANE (SIMULTANEOUS): YUM!

SUPERMAN: I'm sorry, "gentlemen," but the threat is *far* from over.

STUDIO: VOICE BEGINS SOFTLY SINGING, "WHO'S AFRAID OF VIRGINIA WOOLF"

BESS: It isn't? (STARTLED) What do you mean?

LOIS LANE (MYSTERIOUS): Who can tell which plutocrat's hands...are in which man's deep pockets?

SUPERMAN: I mean a terrible threat still remains—to *me*—and, oh yes, to you and to the entire world. Even as we drink, Adam Miller is busy building a deadly green ooozonator!

JIMMY OLSEN (HYPNOTICALLY): Oo-zoo-*zoo*-nator.

LOIS LANE: A threat, Martha? Hunh? (HOPEFULLY)

SUPERMAN: Yes, when you die, George, I'm going to burn all but 2 of your letters—and historians will never ever know why. (CRESCENDO) Then, I'm going to *plant* a cherry tree! Right there in the old garbanzo bean!

LOIS LANE: You're going to get it, Martha.

SUPERMAN: Careful, baby...I'll rip you to pieces.

LOIS LANE: You aren't man enough...you haven't got the guts.

SUPERMAN: Total war?

END.

120 DAYS IN THE FBI
My Untold Story
by Jane Eyre

1

As my powers begin their final waning, I slowly approach the magnificent kingdom in which, assuredly, I will be gloriously reunited with beloved Rochester. I've long ceased regretting my youthful folly as an employee of the American government, and as self-styled, and largely inept, counterspy. However, a deep shame recently overcame me about my unbroken silence on this bizarre and dubious period of my life. Chiefly, fear of nextworld consequences of such a festering secret leads me to take goose quill in hand now to depict these uncanny events of my past—or strangest of truths be told, of a future-yet-to-come.

It happened immediately after quitting Thornfield hall, all this many lo mein ago: fleeing graver danger than the quite literary mad-wife-in-attic scenario. For I *was* tempted by Rochester's insidiously seductive wish, expressed nearly as a command, that I go abroad as his mistress—pampered, spoiled, *worshipped*. I could only allow the faintest accounts of such failings into my original autobiography, for fear that miscomprehending younger readers would suddenly find themselves swaying their own hips mightily.

Noiselessly oiling the locks, I slipped away one bleak dawn without a sound, and with no destination in mind. Once again giving myself over to trust in a merciful God, and in my own bounteous and remarkably steadfast good luck. For how many others of my acquaintance, purer, more deserving (and a whole lot comelier, *dearest Helen*) had already perished from terrible plagues, sheer frustration or miserable privation.

I skirted fields, and hedges, and lanes, till after sunrise. I believe it was a lovely summer morning; I know my shoes, which I had put on when I left the house, were soon wet with dew. But I looked neither to rising sun, nor smiling sky, nor wakening nature.

No reflection was to be allowed now; not one glance was to be cast back to the past; not even one forward. The first was a page so heavenly sweet—so deadly sad—that to read one line of it would dissolve my courage and break down my energy. The last one was an awful blank: something like the world when the deluge was gone by.

Birds began singing in brake and copse: birds were faithful to their mates; birds were emblems of love. What was I? In the midst of my pain of heart, and frantic effort of principle, I abhorred myself. I had no solace from self-approbation: none even from my self-respect.

I had injured—wounded—left my master. I was hateful in my own eyes. Still I could not turn, nor retrace one step. Grief must have led me on. I was weeping wildly as I walked along my solitary way; fast, fast I went like one delirious.

A weakness, beginning inwardly, extending to the limbs seized me, and I fell: I lay on the ground for a long while, pressing my face to the wet turf. I had a vague dread that wild cattle might be near, or that some sportsman or poacher might discover me. Finally a long stupor overtook me.

Can you imagine my dread and astonishment, dear reader, at awakening in what I soon discovered was Washington D.C. in the year 1969? My first chaotic impressions were of monstrously tall and foreboding buildings which seemed designed for swarming populations of overdressed miscreants. Huge metal transports came hurtling toward me like stallions, carrying within glassy-eyed, gin-toting lunatics.

Some of the swiftly striding passersby gawked or laughed outright at my "quaint" garb, but the majority ostentatiously ignored me. One kindly woman timidly tossed paper money. Oddly, a group of ragamuffin gypsies, tattered and multicolored versions of myself, burned frankincense at my feet while brandishing heavenly blue cornflowers and ringing little bells.

Desperately, I searched this scene, which at first I took to be a dream—or delirious glimpse into life on a distant astral body—seeking a sign of grace or divine intervention. Then I noticed that the edifice directly ahead, unlike all the others, was a low brick building, with handsome marble columns and promenades: it conveyed the familiar air of London's showiest establishments (and, indeed, all the paintings inside were of men in periwigs, in faux imperial sagacity).

The entrance announced in elegant, gold letters, FBI: an engraved scroll inside listed the offices of the executives, including one Mr. Aloysius Rochester. In unutterable confusion, I yearned to take this as a favorable portent, even providential, yet dared not. Still, I clung to the thought that my cold and desolate existence might somehow arrive at a more blessed state, although the ecstasy of serving Mr. Rochester was plainly extinguished forever.

In barely suppressed fear and desperation, I entered the haunted marble palace. A toothy, gold-bedecked and buxom blond, virtually lost behind a vast, shiny desk, earnestly greeted me with a bevy of "thee's" and "thou's." Evidently, this perky procuress mistook me for a member of the Friends' Society, due, I believe, to my long grey cloak and absence of facial war paint.

This venerable institution was eager to employ more of my kind, proclaimed the permanently smiling functionary. (Perhaps she was afflicted with a rare muscular disorder; more probably, I imagined her simply of marriageable age.) They keenly wished to gratify the country's new President, himself a Quaker: Mr. Imperious Hawk, who owned either the building or the actual boulevard.

She assumed I had come about the position advertised in "the Moonie paper," so I simply "worked it," as Tyrone would have said: thus initiating a series of interviews with portly gentlemen. Ere long, I underwent a rigor-ous written examination on the topic of "manifest destiny," which I swiftly intuited had something to do with unrepentant slaughtering of Indians and Mexicans. An obscure inquiry into the place of birds in a sport—"Down Jones Golf," if I recall—provoked the condescending observation that, doubtless, gaming ran counter to my ecclesiastical bent.

Happily, the electrical gadget which they hired me to operate several weeks later was simply controlled by a single flick of the wrist—you need not take care about cutting off your fingers, as with the ill-designed spinning jenny which wretched girls of my day had to endure. You may have guessed it, dear reader: I was the new SHREDDER at the FBI.

One fellow employee passed the curious remark early on that I seemed uniquely suited for the job. "It's like you're always erasing yourself anyways," she momentarily mused. At first, I *was* famished for reams of paper to devour. Plentiful documents passed into the monster's maws. There was a war going on somewhere at the outskirts of the empire; they told me foreign agents were everywhere.

2

My Quaker identification proved providential indeed. I was directed to a comfortable and congenial boarding house, full of highly stimulating men and women of the faith. Each night, after a hearty supper, we engaged in a second type of sumptuous and immensely reassuring repast. The attractive, if determinedly overstuffed living room qua library positively rang with lively metaphysical and political discussion, typically on the ethics of bearing witness in an age of barbarism.

Nowhere else in this thickly slick, capital city, or truthfully in all my prior experiences, had I encountered anyone even remotely as contemplative as these new comrades. Naturally, I was quite disturbed when many vitriolically denounced the Vietnam War. But I remained silent, as an alien must—it was established that I hailed from Saskatchewan: at least according to the fake passport which Anna had slipped into the pocket of my simple frock one night after I first arrived, and which proved crucial to securing my new employment.

Several weeks later, I was unexpectedly introduced to Mr. Aloysius Rochester: "quel porker!" as one appealing "hippie chick" on the telly might have saucily described this lecherous gentleman. I had to scoff at my own silly superstitions regarding *my* Mr. Rochester's mystical capabilities to penetrate the veil of time. Oddly though, on that very day, documents began arriving of a different and more alarming nature—*because I could understand them.*

The issue was internal black dissidents. First came a memo with a curious justification for wiretapping Dr. Martin Luther King's phone (news that was just now emerging, years after his murder) on the grounds that two of his aides were Communists—did they believe these men resided with the Kings? Then I was absolutely horrified to discover that the FBI was systematically assassinating leaders of the Black Panther Party.

One infiltrator's report told about how the FBI COINTELPRO had successfully neutralized the coalition between the Panthers and the Student Nonviolent Coordinating Committee, instigated by Mr. Hoover's paranoia of black Americans, using slander tactics similar to earlier ones which divided the supporters of Malcolm X and the Socialist Workers Party. But the Panthers were gaining respect in the black community across the country since 1967 when they began organizing a free breakfast program for children, and offering free health care to ghetto residents.

So FBI agents created a blood feud with the United Slaves. They arranged for Nick Galt's informers in the United Slaves to assassinate Alprentice Carter, the Panthers' Los Angeles minister of defense, and John Huggins, the deputy minister of information. Although the FBI was taking great care to frame Geronimo Pratt for murder, their usual mode was unfocussed direct attack: machine gun down as many leaders as possible.

The FBI arranged for the December, 1969 raid on the Chicago Panthers headquarters in which Fred Hampton and Mark Clark had been killed by the Chicago Police. The FBI informed the police that the Panthers possessed numerous guns and explosives, and they would shoot any police officer who entered the building. The report concluded by noting that a nameless agent had gotten this idea from watching an unidentified early Chicago gangland movie.

I believed these accounts intuitively, or should I say experientially, due to the many disheartening scenes I had already witnessed of the treatment of severely under-compensated black employees, who performed all manual labor for the elaborately Byzantine government offices. I had oft observed that the white lords expected a certain shuffling attitude as debris was disappeared, doors held open, toilets plunged. The black people working there tended to have perpetually vacant grins on their otherwise expressionless faces—as if to suggest that nothing pleased them more than to exude false warmth for their powerful and viciously indifferent masters.

In fact, I remember how astonished and gratified I was to first realize that slavery had actually been abolished in the states. Late one rainy Saturday night, my friend Anna took me to an elegant dancing pavilion (she referred to it as a "bi after-hours club") in the predominantly black section, which seemed to encompass virtually the whole metropolis (all the government bigwigs lived in faraway "Virgin," a grassy area). Throughout a sylvan summer's night, I was spellbound beyond imagination by the glorious, jazzy dancing of these beautiful people.

The rhythms of the music, the glistening bodies and brilliantly colored rainments flashing and swirling encompassed everything, the very boundaries of consciousness. After awhile, Anna impetuously led me by the hand onto the crowded dance floor. From this true perspective, these were absolutely the least enchained people of any I'd ever seen.

Moving harmoniously, Anna's unfettered long blond hair swayed energetically; her characteristic sweet and wry smile remained fixed. Waves of ardor ran through us all, as Alicia Bridges was singing, *"I love the night life, I like to boogie…"* and colored spotlights from high above showered the early morning atmosphere with iridescent dew. Fade in a harmonic pastoral about a love train going off to Africa.

I took a sniff from the little glass bottle being passed around—a form of liquid snuff mayhaps, or palliating spirits against the effects of intensive physical exertion. The world lurched dramatically, flowing in slow motion that was somehow faster too: years seemed to fly by. Just then, a startled, and I would venture, bemused fellow employee (actually, a sub-contracted janitor as I was to learn later) waved gaily at me; Tyrone gracefully glided by with his handsome young male partner.

Tyrone looked so enchantingly happy that I wanted to cry. Immediately, I experienced a thrilling and overwhelming feeling of freedom: a new sensation, I realized in that instant, is not vouchsafed to everyone. It was accompanied by an instantaneous, firm conviction which I expressed to myself as, *from this point on, it doesn't matter so much what happens to me.*

The radical disjunction between Tyrone's workplace and real life dispositions felt immensely significant, practically rendering redundant that moment's inevitable lightning: the nightclub throbbing to the thunder became a spectacular and eternal tableau vivant. I wished to shout to Anna, Tyrone and to everyone present *I'm like you, I understand.* I had a wild impulse to rush over and stare into Tyrone's eyes, where I felt a certainty of seeing my own soul's reflection.

And why not? Didn't I apprehend, *and* comprehend, the subterranean sources of oppression which fed this exuberant paean to life. How keenly I knew the want of independence over even my own movements. How well schooled my silent endurance of miserable misers whose sole interest in me was as cipher in their account book of unhallowed profits.

Lifting my hand to return Tyrone's greeting, I hoped I was somehow telepathically communicating this onrush of sentiments, as I later had reason to believe possible—but I learned, not by dint of the will. (Anna was so funny, joking about the oddity of having a religious experience "on poppers.") Little could I realize, however, that Tyrone was soon to become a major force in my American career.

3

I had invited Tyrone to share my bratwurst and cole slaw lunch on the morrow; he brought organic pomegranate juice. We ate at a nearby park, under beautiful pink and rose cherry trees. Stately swans graced the lovely lake; from the far shore beckoned a once pristine gazebo.

When Tyrone arrived, I was reading a biography of his hero, John Brown, slightly hidden behind a bulky *Reader's Digest* "Condensed Books" including the supposedly amusing *Mrs. 'Arris Goes to Paris*. Tyrone was toting a hefty novel called *Middlemarch*, which he termed a superb dissection of middle and upper class mechanisms of rationalization.

Tyrone explained that he could only afford to attend Howard University part-time. As an orphan, I murmured, college was out of the question—and where I came from, flatly *not* an option for women. Our conversation turned toward the light side; altogether I felt Tyrone was extremely simpatico (a word Anna used to describe our own affinities).

Indeed, I couldn't shake the sensation that somehow I knew him in another life—how could that be the past?—which daily grew more unreal, as I had disciplined myself never to think of it (except when wishing upon the first evening star). Happily, Tyrone attended our next study group, where Roger, his old "coalition buddy," was speaking as a founder of Liberation News Service. Coincidentally, Roger was also Anna's "ex" and first lover—she termed it the "obligatory incest law."

Roger detailed the FBI's overall policy to "disrupt or neutralize, ridicule or discredit" progressive organizations. Typically, agent provocateurs would infiltrate a group and urge reckless, extreme actions, by whipping up fear that fascism was right around the corner—"easy enough to credit," many murmured sympathetically.

Until the Freedom of Information Act was passed a few years ago, investigators had to rely even more heavily on "internal leaks." Were Roger's quick sidelong glances to Tyrone and Anna merely my fancy? And didn't that non-nonchalant trio then assiduously avoid looking in my direction?

I was shocked to learn that at least half our core study group had been or were currently under government surveillance. Some had requested their FBI files. But the few documents which ever arrived were so full of black marks that only an occasional word or phrase remained visible, like "Hollywood gossip columnist Joyce Haber extracted."

In fact, later that night we improvised a merry MAD LIBS party game, filling in erasures. "We need a transgressive verb here," Anna would call out, martini held high, "or a saucy adjective for pigs!" The game ended in raucous dancing, when someone put on a Martha and the Vandellas record and turned out the lights.

Afterwards, chatting with Tyrone on the chintz divan about Mrs. Gaskell's exquisite, class conscious novels, Roger and Anna casually wafted by. Pulling up old oaken chairs, Anna looked away disingenuously, while Tyrone quietly commented that being inside the FBI, seat of such villainous power, would certainly provide someone with a unique opportunity to perform an invaluable service for "the people." He didn't say it with quotes around it, dear reader, but that was the only way I could hear such abstract rhetoric.

Roger had been monitoring Heritage Foundation cultural policy meetings in which they were planning vicious retaliation against scholars and artists who had been articulating vital issues of the decade—abortion, civil liberties, the genocide of indigenous tribes of Latin America. Soon, the government would only fund culture that its politicians (never mind trusting subversive artists with such judgments!) deemed "mainstream quality."

These "upcoming buzz words," Anna predicted, would rapidly supersede "cultural democracy," to which some lip service was just now beginning to be paid. The ultimate goal? To ensure that all individuals who become artists possess trust funds of one million dollars minimally, following the post-war European model. (Was Anna trying to impress Roger?—did her heart still beat faster at his softcore patter?)

Ranting bitterly about their labor policies, Roger pointed out that Heritage Foundation co-founders Joseph Coors and Paul Weyrich had long been associated with the notorious John Birch Society. Weyrich founded the Free Congress Foundation, which hired a convicted Nazi war criminal to coordinate its European activities. That started Anna in on the gaggles of Nazis who were imported to D.C. right after the war to help organize the fledgling CIA, cauldron of pure evil, etc.

I remained silent. But I vividly remembered shredding a proposal that Weyrich was apparently discreetly circulating, calling for the federal government to secretly lace illegal drugs with substances like rat poison and release them into the black market. It was one of my numerous occasions wondering, if by any remote chance, this could be some sort of inconceivably tasteless joke.

Further, Roger named a sleazy character, Richard Mellon Scaife, as the largest single donor to the Foundation. Smiling acerbically, I related in a neutral tone how I once overheard Scaife maliciously growling at a dignified *Washington Post* reporter who was questioning him about Vietnam, "You fucking Communist cunt, get out of here!" Tyrone shot a glance at me, inexpressibly peculiar, and quite incomprehensible.

His glance seemed to take and make note of every point in my shape, face and dress; for it traversed all, quick, keen as lightening. Tyrone's lips parted, as if to speak: but he checked the coming sentence, whatever it was. Suddenly, I felt certain this whole discussion had been constructed, maybe even rehearsed, as part of a concerted campaign to solicit my services as a mole in the FBI.

4

I trusted these zealous friends, with my life if necessary—that wasn't the issue. Forthright and unswerving in their beliefs, they had a subtle and profound understanding of the body politic. Most important, their actions conformed to lofty thinking: a rare characteristic which must always stand in my highest regard.

Nevertheless, it was precisely such passionate, wild-eyed (and in the case of Roger, frizzy-haired!) idealism, frequently mistaken by outsiders for cynicism, that might well lead to the destruction of my small measure of sanity. Perhaps I had already fallen into the grips of sheer paranoia. Except, weren't these the very people who had taught me that you can't be *too* paranoid, if you're conscientiously trying to do right in this blighted era.

Nobody had exactly asked me to become a spy. Nevertheless, one night at dinner I introduced the topic, mentioning how impossible it would be to conceive of spying on an employer. "Again, speaking for myself," I concluded, looking into each one's eyes, "the most I can imagine is inadvertently repeating a phrase or two, say at the dinner table, that I happened to have stumbled upon in the course of daily work—hopefully some good might germinate from that."

"It very well could, at that, Jane Pear," Roger casually remarked. Yes, dear reader that was my name, ever since the extremely blond receptionist at the FBI had made the initial mistake. Believe me, how sharply I would have corrected her, had I known then to what moronic and infantile "jokes" this nomenclature would subject me to from would-be, witty adolescent males of all ages. Anna changed the subject to granola muffins.

I was pleased to have been as forthright as possible under the circumstances, a state to which I felt naturally inclined, also due to lengthy subsistence within a sea of hypocrites. Anyway, I probably hadn't implicated us in a conspiracy—the government was zealously identifying and prosecuting "dissidents" everywhere.

Of course, what I yearned to be forthright *about* was that I had actually known Mr. Karl Marx slightly. In fact, I'd been a recipient of many courteous, absent-minded nods in the British Museum, during respites from his diligent toils. Once we two had even exchanged pleasantries about Saint-Simon's personal peccadilloes.

Now it was a kind of permanent shock and delight to me that this serious, hoary-haired young scholar was viewed worldwide as the very fount of cataclysmic beneficence or evil. Parenthetically, dear reader, Mr. Marx and I shared the significance of the date 1848, which saw the publication of my own humble memoir (under the curious pseudonym Currier Bell) as well as his earth-shattering though then rather neglected *Communist Manifesto*.

Meanwhile, our study group was focusing on the history of slavery, starting with early rebellions unrecorded in any textbook. One vivid and highly memorable article by the historian Howard Zinn contained first person accounts of the condition of slave ships, which were characteristically covered in mucous and blood; many "frenzied Africans" took their own lives aboard these floating prison/slaughterhouses.

I heard much about recent summer "race riots," and their forerunners in furious frustrated urban explosions, especially in the '40s when all Negro soldiers were sent to boot camp in the deep South. We dissected the *Kerner*

Report: 1968 Report of the National Advisory Committee on Civil Disorders, concurring that its findings were astonishingly radical coming from a motley group of businessmen and politicians who had barely been liberals before beginning their exhaustive, nation-wide interviewing.

The Commission, for example, called for the immediate creation of 2 million new jobs, divided equally between the public and private sectors. It suggested massive public housing construction, beginning with 600,000 new units in the first year. Similar lofty gestures were made in other areas of institutionalized racism, like education and police brutality.

None of these proposals would ever vaguely approach implementation, our group insisted. They called the *Kerner Report* a "testimony to the ill will of those in power toward rectifying their own most manifest abuses." They truly despised capitalism.

5

Dear reader, I don't wish you to think of me as consummately consumed in gloom. My job was undemanding, and I spent much time with Anna and others, walking, gossiping, eating, going to record and book stores, and very often indulging my strongest passion—movies.

Happily, there was a heavenly ornate, rococo repertory theater right around the corner, with frequently changing classic Hollywood and foreign films. In this instance, my total ignorance was readily explicable: there were no movie theaters for hundreds of miles where I grew up. Friends eagerly filled me in on cinema's history and finest achievements.

I viewed movies with such unnatural raptness, perhaps attempting symbolic mastery over my actual dilemmas, that I was always amazed my entire masquerade wasn't quite transparent. To be transported again to a time and place not of my choosing (or understanding)—let us just say that I had trouble viewing films as fictitious. I was a sucker for sci-fi flicks, like *2001*, and particularly, as Anna insisted, for the sentimental, or "schlock."

A few truly distinguished movies affected me profoundly. The first was *Pinky*, a rare treatment of the subject of "passing," and from 1949! The story begins with a deeply confused Jeanne Crain returning home to see her grandmother (Ethel Waters) who, on meager laundress' wages, had sent Pinky up North to graduate from nursing school.

Pinky is quickly reminded of her place, in grimly realistic, mercifully brief vignettes of razors and would-be rapist policemen. But the setting itself has a mitigating effect, as if the cast has stepped out of the pages of a handsomely illustrated novel. The artfully stylized, painted backdrop to the humble yet homey rural dwelling (Ethel Barrymore's graciously decrepit plantation in the distance) suggests more harmonious forms, and the possibility of classical themes.

Pinky has a wonderful happy ending too: the unusually strong interracial friendship between the two old women endures. Partly in payment for nursing services, Ethel Barrymore wills the granddaughter Pinky the plantation, with instructions to use it sagaciously. Embracing her own identity, Pinky decides to stay and establish a day care center and nursing school for her people.

Afterwards, over a late night schnitzel and beer, I commented on the remarkable ending, pivoting around Pinky's rejection of romantic love in the distinctly tangible form of handsome, white, kindly, soon-to-be affluent young doctor, and in favor of higher moral imperatives. But the doctor's scheme was so severely "retro," Anna proclaimed: the beleaguered couple moves to Denver, he supports her, she continues passing.

The fiancé represented Pinky's "last temptation," Anna argued. Of course his plan was totally unrealistic: taking into account neither the question of children nor that Pinky's legal battles with the blood heirs had already made her notorious in the national Negro newspapers. Anna loved the movie's focus on how Pinky's valiantly attempted mediations of intensely thorny contradictions affected her heroic and holy grandmother: "where class, race and gender intersected mightily with ethics, duty and desire."

Then Anna (whose favorite uncle had been fatally blacklisted) bitterly recounted a morality tale concerning the compliance of *Pinky*'s director, Mr. Elia Kazan, with the evil HUAC hearings. Their satanic ringleader, Joe McCarthy, used to force victims to publicly denounce one another, even though he had all their names and was already persecuting them. Anyone who refused was blacklisted; a number were jailed (some, members of the European émigré community, I'm proud to report).

Mr. Kazan had established an important career in movies with social messages, like *Gentleman's Agreement*, *Viva Zapata* and the steamy *A Streetcar Named Desire*. It had been believed that his defiance would constitute a major setback to the hearings. Instead of condemning the proceedings, Mr. Kazan's full-page ad in the *New York Times* urged cooperation (earning undying enmity of former friends): addressing liberals as if they were ignorant dupes of communists, as the real threat to freedom of speech, rather than the witch hunts themselves.

How I yearned "to share" with Anna that I came from a time and place in merry old England not so far removed from literal witch hunts. I remember reading about a stooped-over old woman in Hastings who, refusing to remain silent at her neighbors' tauntings, was accused of assuming the form of a cat and causing lameness in children. In my day, the north of England was still notorious for its witch doctors, or *cunning men* as they were called: when medicine failed, they were consulted to counter the curse which had presumably caused the ailment.

Anna's Elia Kazan account deliberately raised crucial ethical questions. But I had no inkling that meeting George X. Bushman at the water cooler (where he democratically mixed with us "proles") would so soon put me to the acid test, in the sketchy and ludicrous Affair of the Red Panties, starring Mr. Bushman's rowdy "sidekick," Alfredo Noriega.

6

Predictably, one week after I came to have limited access to classified information, Tyrone passed on a request: Roger wished to see the file of Geronimo Pratt, a Vietnam veteran and Southern California Black Panther leader, who the FBI was in the process of framing for murder.

Early on, I had told them all about shredding a document, which stated, "the LAPD won't tell the jury that Olsen positively identified at least three others suspects before he identified Pratt," and that occurred only *after* Mr. Pratt's connections to the Panthers were thoroughly explained to this eager-to-please eyewitness. Further, the LAPD was planning to testify that the gun found in Pratt's apartment was the murder weapon, "even though the barrel was missing."

My current augmented spying potential arose from helping grateful Mr. Bushman out of a perplexing pickle. Early one morning, he arrived in the company of a swarthy, well-dressed but obviously confused individual. Mr. Noriega appeared to hanker (hunker?) after me, or maybe the man was just under the influence of laudanum. In any case, at my desk, he began eagerly sniffing the air and staring quizzically, as if he thought he should recognize me, doubtless from some subservient position in his younger years.

I smiled continuously, as my job description seemed to demand (and as American females are presumably instructed at their mothers' bosoms). It was my unwritten duty to tidy up the penthouse suite, with its well-stocked liquor cabinet and palpable amenities. That evening, a birthday party was to be held there for "Tricky Dick's" dog, Chesty—typically, I hadn't a clue if that was a joke—away from the prying eyes of the White House staff.

Seated on opposite sides of the penthouse, the two men were frozen in an unforgettable pose, which might well serve as the very definition of "lurid." Mr. Noriega had his pants open, and the painted green fingernails of his right hand were avidly yet somehow inattentively rubbing his bright red underwear. In a hoarse whisper, he was virtually barking a ritualized lament: "Don't admit it to Red China. Tickiticata...."

Mr. Bushman, on the contrary, had no expression whatsoever (only his face wasn't caked in white like his friend's). Oddly, this statesman appeared to be doing and thinking absolutely nothing, like an expensive machine that had been inadvertently clicked off. Dear reader, Edgar Allen Poe's famous cataleptic Lady Madeleine Usher swiftly came to mind—another meshuggah aristocrat, as Roger would say.

Mr. Bushman was commonly perceived as insensate, functioning as an embodiment of the drives of his social class. Even initially, I admit finding this palsied patrician's patronizing noblesse oblige slightly refreshing after the aristocracy's usual blank indifference or mildly dyspeptic hostility. Indeed, I wasn't surprised to hear that Mr. Bushman was related to Britain's royal family, but I couldn't understand the awe and pleasure in my co-worker's voice, a tone which I previously had thought reserved, and rightly so, for movie stars and musicians.

In any case, I helped the dumbstruck duo to exit the building unnoticed—the mere existence of the freight elevator seemed to greatly astonish them—after assisting Mr. Noriega in buttoning up his gummy pants. The very next day, I was informed of my raise. Also, I was to be accessible whenever Mr. Bushman was in the building; usually that merely meant soothing ruffled feathers.

I put Tyrone off, dreading the central moral showdown which I knew was coming. Although I prided myself on facing such conundrums unflinchingly, I must confess in those days all I wanted was to incessantly escape into the movies. Ironically, it was a knockout double feature of *Picnic* and *Splendor in the Grass* which led to my own heightened sensory experiences (to "free love," I joyously confess): in turn occasioning a fresh, sober assessment of duty and desire.

Four breathtaking and luscious young stars trembling and cooing in back-to-back technicolor lust. Tawny teenage Natalie Wood literally driven mad with unsatisfied cravings for sturdy and sleek Warren Beatty. Never before had desire felt so natural and lovely, its repression so sinister and deadly.

The last straw came in *Picnic*'s deflated climax. In a drunken holiday frenzy, frustrated Rosalind Russell rips the clothes off ripe and virile drifter William Holden, object of budding Kim Novak's ooziest desires ("Get it, girl!" Tyrone merrily exclaimed). Was I destined to become like that desperate schoolteacher?

"The evidence of inaction," Tyrone proclaimed grandly, "is worth two carpe-diems!" Then he informed me that his childhood buddy Carl, a beautiful bisexual man, was currently in town on shore leave (Tyrone swore that, alas, they'd never had carnal relations). Tyrone had already made plans for us all to go dancing next weekend.

It turned out to be a wondrous, unforgettable night. Most of our "bar crowd" were there (many on mushrooms), and I experienced an energized yet deeply relaxing sense of belonging. (Besides, Anna and Tyrone repeatedly proclaimed how "hot" I looked.) After dancing for hours, Carl and I went back to Tyrone's temporarily vacated, champagne-stocked apartment.

At last, I was set free! Kissing Carl, at first I closed my eyes and tried to pretend he was Mr. Rochester. But Tyrone's, *whoops,* Carl's café-au-lait skin was too silken; he was too handsome, ardent, and sweet. I opened my eyes.

Soon those faint images of my master vanished along with my inhibitions. Carl's lithe torso was solidly muscular, a divine classical instrument. All night long, I experienced what the philosophers must have meant when they spoke of bliss.

The next day, I woke up with the conviction that I would help Roger, and attempt to Xerox the Geronimo Pratt file. Not out of guilt, I reasoned. Only slightly due to a sense that pleasure must be paid for, mostly because of feeling that now I had nothing left to lose.

I simply had no idea how long I would remain in my present, or in *any* life-situation. With a vague presentiment of some major transformation, I didn't want to leave anything undone which I might regret. And in that frame of mind, I rolled over against Carl's beautiful slumbering body, caressing and licking his exquisite thighs.

7

Carl returned to the base in Bremerton, Washington, where he ran the canteen, a sinecure secured by an ardent admirer. With only a year left, he was certain he wouldn't be sent to Vietnam: before that, Carl had been seriously considering going AWOL. Asking me to write him (which, of course, I avidly did), Carl reiterated that as Tyrone had doubtless informed me, he had at least one girl and guy in every port.

I readied myself to seize any spontaneous Xeroxing opportunity that might arise. Mr. Bushman often phoned at odd hours for a personal errand—to make a late night run for a cube of ambergris for his secretary-mistress, or for some Polident-lite for his wife, Tabitha (whom I, at first, like everyone else, mistook for Mr. Bushman's "well-preserved" mother).

Soon, such a request came. Mr. Bushman was about to fly off to Japan. His stomach was quite upset—in fact, he had just vomited all over the Japanese ambassador. I was to lay in a store of Pepto-Bismol and brioches, which he would pick up on his way to the airport in the morning.

Tabitha was staying home in rural Virgin (where, strange to report, they still hunted foxes) to enter a quilting bee. Therefore, I was instructed to patronize ersatz antique shops in search of a handsome homemade quilt. "Pricey yet understated," the proud husband roundly remonstrated.

Returning to the office late that night, I deposited my purchases on Mr. Bushman's desk. I figured I may as well "catch up on my Xeroxing" (the phrase I had rehearsed in case anyone was still in the building). Scurrying off to nab that one additional file, suddenly I felt I was moving too furtively.

The image of Nora Charles came to mind, really the divine Myrna Loy—how could I imitate her sang-froid? Trying to remember what Anna had told me about "method acting," I sort of sauntered down the hall: bemused Nora, or Myrna, glancing insouciantly hither and yon.

With few lights on, the shadows looked like film noir—artistically shaped geometric forms, eerily looming. I almost convinced myself that I was in a lavish 1930s Park Avenue art deco apartment. How delightful it would be, mused I, to crawl into bed with William Powell.

I entered the Xerox room. Nonchalantly and efficiently, I slipped in the first few pages of the Geronimo Pratt file, which was lodged firmly in my bosom. But as I was reaching for the next batch of documents, I heard voices. The door abruptly opened.

In walked Mr. Bushman with two other gentlemen. As if the film had shifted into slow motion, I turned after an agony of waiting. Freeze-frame: our gazes interlocked. What would imperturbable Nora do at this moment? I longed for an elegant crystal decanter of martinis to divert us all.

Instead, I inquired warmly after Mr. Bushman's intestines. I trusted that the bitter cold wasn't bothersome—shivering slightly, conveniently buttoning up my sweater. Mr. Bushman emitted a brief yet all too detailed account of his bowel inactivity. I remained poised for sympathetic banter.

He was quite pleased with the "earthy" quilt I had selected. Its tawny brown and orange colors reminded him of the high price of genuine marmalade, about which Tabitha had recently informed him, in some detail apparently. While feverishly calculating how to finish copying the Pratt file that night, I couldn't help noticing that one of Mr. Bushman's associates was tall, dark and handsome.

Finally, this gentleman was introduced: Mr. Daniel Ellsberg, a member of a "think tank" (quel misnomer!) which was instrumental in facilitating the annihilation of the indigenous Vietnamese population. When Mr. Bushman alluded to this, Mr. Ellsberg actually blushed—I wondered how he could still be capable of doing so.

Eventually, the trio left (but not before Mr. Bushman heartily extolled the virtues of homemade aspic). At the window, watching Mr. Bushman climb into his limousine and wave to someone outside the frame, I heaved a sigh of relief. However, just as I was about to insert the file back into the locked cabinet, Mr. Daniel Ellsberg walked into the room, large as life.

The name GERONIMO PRATT was plainly visible. Idiot!—why hadn't I covered it? Quickly, I wondered what they did to aliens in American prisons: would I be permitted to call Anna before the first hosing?

Mr. Ellsberg was starting *at*, practically though me: that already distinguished him from all upper-echelon males I had ever encountered in this building. In my best Nora Charles manner, I began lightly joking that our work load was so heavy, we clericals had even been considering unionizing—hoping to throw him onto another track, or to derail him entirely.

Despite my terror, I found myself drawn to Mr. Ellsberg, vaguely confusing him with the debonair William Powell. (Their moustaches seemed to blur.) Finally, a slow smile broke through Mr. Ellsberg's intense gaze and he remarked, "You know, Miss Pear, I'm only a consultant. In fact, I don't approve of everything the FBI is doing, and for that reason, I could never work here."

In singular, heartfelt tones, he added, "We've all got to fight for justice in our own ways." I demurred, jamming the file back into the cabinet. He offered me a ride home, if I was finished with my *work*, he declared with peculiar emphasis.

On the drive, we chatted pleasantly about the band "Strawberry Alarm Clock." With an inexplicable grin, Mr. Ellsberg mentioned that Al, and particularly Tipper Gore were "deadheads." There was a final, odd joke about stewed secrets in a pickled pumpkin patch.

The next day, Roger took me out to lunch and I handed over the Xeroxes. I told him this had to be my first and last caper. I was simply too timid—obviously, I hadn't seen enough *Thin Man* movies, I joked. Roger smiled, and ordered chocolate mousse for our desserts.

What I *didn't* tell Roger, or anyone, concerned the strange time warp which I had just experienced. Walking down marbled FBI corridors, I suddenly saw myself as an old woman: seated in Mr. Rochester's boudoir *(and mine?)*, writing about those selfsame, darkened hallways. I was there, and simultaneously remembering this unholy edifice from long ago.

Superstitiously looking all round, I half expected to hear Mr. Rochester's hearty baritone voice booming out through the chasms of time, "Jane! Jane Pear!" Did this qualify as a premonition? Is it conceivable that I could yet be reunited with my beloved master, after this unique and eternal language adventure of mine?

8

Instead of Xeroxing, now I tried to read every document I could without arousing suspicion, and to carefully commit key phrases to memory. I was back into dropping-hints-around-dinner-table-mode, which my friends seemed willing to accept, at least temporarily.

Mentioning "Operation Hoodwink," I had the piquant pleasure of astonishing the usually well-informed "insider" Roger (who later used this information to gain access to previously closed circles). After more than a little gentle teasing, I revealed that from 1966 through mid-1968, the FBI had been fabricating documents with which they hoped to incite organized crime to retaliate against invented acts of the Communist Party.

I was able to corroborate a rumor that the FBI was currently targeting a Professor Morris Starsky of Arizona State University; he and his wife were presidential electors when the Socialist Workers Party gained a place on the ballot in Arizona in 1968. The FBI had just influenced the State Board of Regents there to "find cause to separate Professor Starsky from the public payroll." Apparently, the FBI was incensed that the SWP was running candidates for office, "and supported such causes as Castro's Cuba and integration problems in the South," as an early memo stated.

We all agreed that the FBI's most infamous and shameful role was its disruption of anti-racist activities. Also well-known to the left were the FBI's frequent refusals to invoke their legal right to protect protesters who were savagely being beaten by police, as in Jackson, Mississippi in 1965—or by mobs, which happened there earlier with the Freedom Riders.

It was perversely gratifying to enlighten Roger about COINTELPRO's success in driving a black minister from the Jackson Human Rights Project, causing him to leave the South altogether. Having sent him a "spurious, threatening letter," they then encouraged school and church officials to file complaints against him based on untruthful charges due to derogatory information the FBI provided.

Clearly, it was only a short while till Roger would again request written evidence of the government's latest villainy. I didn't want to think about that. Or about how eerily I'd been feeling lately—like I wasn't quite real; *as if I wasn't supposed to be there.* Needless to say, Anna and I were escaping to the movies virtually hourly, as happy as clams.

All too often, our study group discussed the complexities of coalition politics, and the bizarre in-fights among various sects. I knew that as a gay man, Tyrone would be denied membership in the Communist Party and all Marxist-Leninist, including multitudinous Maoist ones, but not Trotskyite groups, like the SWP. Viewing "sexual deviance" as the product of "bourgeois decadence," even more bizarrely, they believed it would simply vanish when capitalism did.

I began to feel that I honestly couldn't comprehend anything fundamental about this era: the more I learned, the more enigmatic and profoundly self-destructive it all seemed. Although I certainly understood the absolutely rapacious nature of capitalism, I found utterly baffling the hope-lessly unrealistic or self-styled utopian thinking by some of its opponents, who could otherwise be so ruthless and pragmatic. Furthermore, how did such a cogent critique of the state's oppression coexist with some of them professing frankly puritanical self-repression?

Speaking of sex, Carl returned to D.C. for a glorious weekend—or more precisely, a thrilling looooong Saturday night. I had an almost pre-scient sensation that I would never see Carl again. Not that I let myself dwell on that—or on the distant past, and certainly not on my wishes for the future. Dissociation had asserted itself as the norm, a regimen.

Roger finally asked for the Jean Seberg file, no small matter to me. Jean Seberg was a lovely and fine young actress who was being unmerci-fully harassed by the FBI for her $10,000 donation to the Black Panthers. A communiqué from the Los Angeles Racial Squad alleged Seberg was a "beautiful, internationally known white American actress with extremist relationships, and reportedly a sex pervert."

Consequently, the bureau busily planted rumors in both the tabloids and mainstream press that the baby which Seberg was expecting was fathered by a Panther leader and not by her husband, the well-known writer and French diplomat, Romain Gary. (They were implementing similar tactics with Jane Fondu, another young actress, but lamented that she appeared considerably less vulnerable.)

Roger coveted a copy of the memo in which the FBI advised waiting two months to break this story to gossip columnists: Seberg's pregnancy would be obvious then, and these rumors most effectively "cheapen her image." A phrase in itself so "juicily tabloid" that Roger had high hopes he could tempt the liberal press to reprint it. I equivocated uneasily; he waited.

One night, the Pancake House was immersed in an odd blue haze. Anna, Roger and Tyrone were discussing *Rebel Without a Cause*, *Breathless* and the delicious Cassavetes feature, *Shadows*, as self-conscious admixtures of American and European film making. For a light-headed, confusing moment, I thought they were talking about me.

Anna repeated our original dialog on seeing *Breathless*, when I termed it "the downside of existentialism." Its characters seemed under a compulsion to act, although they had no moral or emotional basis from which to do so. In the end, Jean Seberg informs on her cop-killing lover (whom the police then shoot in the back, running down the street), apparently due to her lack of sufficient cause *not* to turn him in.

Warning Jean-Paul Belmondo about the imminent arrival of the police, Seberg remarks that she called them to prove to herself she isn't in love with him. "Perhaps (futilely) trying to demonstrate the existence of genuine feeling—by designing action based on its hypothetical non-existence," I suggested. Even more overt in its existential themes, *Shadows* features a parodic yet erudite discussion at a jazz party about the major precepts of a Jean-Paul Sartre article—one character claims there are none!

I had already been obsessively seeing everything as "existential," ever since reading Simone de Beauvoir's *Memoirs of a Dutiful Daughter*. Although our circumstances were nothing alike, we both had actively rebelled against the historical imperatives locking us into such a narrow range of experience. Simone's father, a lawyer and erstwhile theatrical producer, encouraged her to become a teacher only after he lost all of that aristocratic family's money and could no longer provide a dowry—luckily, she was a member of the very first class at the Sorbonne which admitted women.

What affinity I felt for her precise attention to consciousness evolving in everyday life. In my mental estrangement, I harbored no doubts that Simone and Jean Seberg were bosom friends. On the ride home, I witnessed erudite and quirky dialogs, as the pair drifted down the Seine on a royal barge.

9

By the time we arrived home, I was feeling quite insubstantial, as if I might simply dematerialize. The beautiful blue haze sometimes was like tapioca, sometimes hemp. Impulsively, I blurted out, "I may have to fly back to Saskatchewan soon to see my ailing mother—don't be alarmed if I suddenly vanish."

They all looked at me so strangely, lovingly. Then they began to glow in a variety of brilliantly colored auras: why hadn't I ever noticed? I apologized for procrastinating about the Jean Seberg file; Roger gently indicated there was still plenty of time, but he didn't seem to believe it.

With a warm, strong hug, Anna asked if I would be all right. Did I want to stay overnight with them?—by that point, she had happily moved back in with Roger. Leaving my dear comrades with deep reluctance, vast gratitude and appreciation, I kissed each one on the eyes.

"A halo of sadness fell like a veil upon her." That line from the *Narrative of Sojourner Truth* came to me. Feeling singularly detached yet sentimental, I kissed the Janis Joplin poster, and took a long look around my cozy and monastic room.

That night I never thought to sleep; but slumber fell on me as soon as I lay down in bed. I was transported in thought to the scene of childhood: I dreamt I lay in the red-room at Gateshead; that the night was dark, and my mind impressed with strange fears. The light that long ago had struck me into syncope, recalled in this vision, seemed glidingly to mount the wall, and tremblingly to pause in the center of the obscured ceiling.

I lifted up my head to look: the roof resolved to clouds, high and dim; the gleam was such as the moon imparts to vapours she is about to sever. I watched her come—watched with the strangest anticipation; as though some word of doom were to be written on her disk. She broke forth as never moon yet burst from cloud: a hand first penetrated the sable folds and waved them away.

Then, not a moon, but a white human form shone in the azure, inclining a glorious brow earthward. It gazed and gazed on me. And as Jean Seberg stared, a bright orange and yellow, end-of-the-world backdrop emerged—with its spiky purple plants, a sort of lurid, sci-fi version of my beloved moors.

When the mists cleared, I saw Jean Seberg standing in a stark spotlight over an open grave where her dead baby lay; black was everywhere else. The tiny, very premature baby was absolutely white-skinned. Seberg hysterically and repeatedly pointed that fact out to many swarming members of the press.

Suddenly, it was 9 years later to the day, and I was watching Jean Seberg commit suicide by locking herself in the car and taking pills. I knew her rotting body wouldn't be found for weeks. From the pristine clarity of these gruesome scenes, and my own belief in them, I felt this must be a visitation and no ordinary dream.

That dear baritone voice crying "Jane Pear!" caused an onrush of confusing sentiments. Wanting to follow the master's voice, I wouldn't abandon my friends. How intolerable the notion of never "catching a flick" or going dancing again with Anna and Tyrone.

As my name grew louder, I lay on the ground and fervently prayed for *memory*. I was stubbornly clinging to an idea: don't return to England without a sense of certainty that I would remember my blessed American family.

A weakness, beginning inwardly, extending to the limbs seized me, and I fell: I lay on the ground for a long while, pressing my face to the wet turf. I had a vague dread that wild cattle might be near, or that some sportsman or poacher might discover me. Finally a long stupor overtook me.

Much later, I opened my eyes to find my thoroughly bewildered cousin, Roger St. John, towering above me.

"You don't look anything like *Roger*, thank God," I gasped, "so this ending *isn't* like the *Wizard of Oz*." A vast wave of relief washed over me: not the least of it—I *remembered*. Losing consciousness again, I lapped up sleep like a kitten with fresh milk.

Afterwards, I awakened on my cousin's comfortably brocaded divan. Through dense layers of chintz and gauze, my eyes lit on an ancient oak tree outside the window, which began to gleam supernaturally. Suddenly, I felt wholly convinced that any letters deposited there would somehow find their way to my American friends in another dimension. Reader, I am not embarrassed to report that I still pen such missals to long-departed comrades—and reverently placing them in the hollow, those letters still disappear!

Roger dropped to his knees and gave thanks, at some length I might add, for my successful convalescence. Luxuriating in the wonderfully soft pillows, I felt confident now that my strange journey would someday lead me back to Mr. Rochester. For the time being, I knew my cousin would prove a boon companion—he was kind, intelligent and considering the times, only a tad of a prig.

But here I must stop, dear reader: for all that is yet another story, long ago told.

ONE OR TWO THINGS I KNOW ABOUT KATHY ACKER

On the eve of her death in a Tijuana cancer clinic, her publisher at Grove Press, Ira Silverberg, called again, this time trying to locate Kathy's illegitimate twins: he had been told about them by her cousin, Pooh Kaye, the dancer. Elly Antin answered the phone. After initial incredulity, she kind of thought she remembered hearing something about one of them. (Much of Elly's rich artistic life has entailed creating dazzling and durable superstructures for her own deepest fantasy personae.) *One twin?*

I had known Kathy since we were college freshmen together, and I could assure them both that no such offspring existed. Several days later, Kathy's second husband, Peter Gordon, the composer, emailed a mutual friend inquiring into the whereabouts of said twins, having also talked to Pooh Kaye. Kathy and Peter had lived together for seven years in the '70s, on both coasts (they married about a month before splitting up): the twins allegedly originated prior to their meeting.

I find it remarkable that these individuals, who knew Kathy intimately, should grant even momentary credibility to this tale of the twins. The willingness to suspend disbelief, on the part of people who undoubtedly have a healthy dose of skepticism regarding virtually all other matters, can be seen as a tribute to the urgency of what Kathy represented to all of us. That is, expansive and transformative possibilities, and the primacy of imagination, or the malleability of reality in its mighty wake. (Twins have a definite resonance, being connected to Dionysius and the dual nature of the Roman god Mercurius, a key figure for alchemists. Pindar wrote about twins living one day in the underworld and one in the world above.)

I don't intend to analyze these individuals here, but their reactions seem to speak to complex emotional states at Kathy's death, including an uncharacteristic gullibility, and a desire to perpetuate her legendary status as well as a living connection with her. I myself managed to refrain from embellishing the rumor, though I toyed with the idea of claiming paternity for the late Herbert Marcuse, eminent Marxist philosopher: the original rumor came replete with nameless professor/lover twin progenitor.

Kathy had first moved to San Diego in 1966, after her sophomore year, when she married Bob Acker (an epic in itself, in which he was at the apex of a torrid triangle); Acker, more a self-styled nihilist than a leftist, followed Marcuse from Brandeis to grad school at UCSD. (One of the frequent erroneous biographical "facts" about Kathy is that *she* was "under the mentorship of Herbert Marcuse," as Spencer Dew puts it in the introduction to his 2011, *LEARNING FOR REVOLUTION: The Work of Kathy Acker.*)

In some senses, the twin rumor could appear credible: Kathy was widely experienced (and began having sex very early), extremely sophisticated, mobile, influential in international arts and literary circles. And utterly uncompromising. Kathy's life and work were of a piece in the absolute rigor with which they opposed smothering and authoritarian conventions and platitudinous, bourgeois morality. As the press release for her L.A. memorial at Beyond Baroque so correctly stated:

> A ferocious, brilliant, and groundbreaking artist reflecting and assaulting post-innocence America…Acker was a visionary in the traditions of Rimbaud and Burroughs, dedicated to the possibilities of a revolutionary writing that rages against every authority, fiction, and creed, then keeps on going.

Kathy's writings are deeply involved with *embracing others' experiences,* while rendering and recontextualizing her own within "appropriated" worlds of social and political carnage, but also of a gloriously sustaining literary heritage. (She disliked the term "appropriation": "I just do what gives me most pleasure: write. As the Gnostics put it, when two people fuck, the whole world fucks.") Kathy's carefully constructed public image often seemed wrong, way oversimplified. That was largely due to forces outside her control, such as the otherwise excellent publication *RE/Search*'s ridiculous 1999 *Angry Women* issue. (As if 95% of the world's population isn't in a rage, or wouldn't be if they weren't too exhausted or heavily narcotized.)

Those who were chiefly familiar with the neo-punk or neo-primitive images—who usually hadn't read any of her books—tended to be astonished at Kathy's delicate and well-bred drawing room manners, and formidable conversational skills. These coexisted with many salient qualities, including wildness (à la *Wuthering Heights*); solipsism; a lifetime of thrilling, avaricious reading and passionate intellectual pursuits; obsessive masochistic tendencies, which unfortunately could not always be confined to the sexual realm where they afforded her vast pleasure.

Certainly, dramatically varied life experiences were integral to Kathy's rough evolution from Sutton Place to déclassé Bohemian, in which she plays a heroine straight out of the deepest novelistic traditions of *Moll Flanders, Vanity Fair*, and pre-eminently, the Brontës. After her marriage to Acker, Kathy basically had no contact with her family—before that, they had sent her to the finest (and Waspiest) New York private girls' schools, and otherwise ignored her—till many years later when she inherited a good deal of money from her grandmother. This era included multiple abortions, and visits to "free clinics" (along with occasional futile phone calls to her mother asking for money to go to a doctor), and way too many prolonged, painful outbreaks of pelvic inflammatory disease, requiring much bed rest—one direct link to Kathy's subsequent love of bodybuilding and motorcycle riding.

Speaking of the legend, her employment then was largely in the wacky world of "adult entertainment." In San Diego, she rather happily worked as a stripper in several downtown joints and elsewhere (a van took them on a nightly circuit). Most of the people we knew who were out of grad school

(Kathy lasted about five minutes in that stultifying atmosphere) had unenviably hideous jobs, like room service waiter or editing slick and bogus textbooks for CRM, publisher of *Psychology Today* ad nauseum. Kathy, a.k.a. "Target," would do an interpretative strip to "Ché," by Ornette Coleman I believe, after carefully explaining to the audience of mostly sailors who Ché was and just why he was so venerable.

Earlier, in New York, Kathy had made a few porn films and worked for awhile in a "live sex show" (i.e. simulated) in Times Square. This gig consisted of composing then acting out skits with her live-in lover Lenny, such as the perennially popular, dastardly therapist/ingenue patient. But Kathy quit those jobs when she was driven into a state of unbearable nightmares about leering men. In this period, Kathy was writing under the noms de plume of RIP-OFF RED, girl detective, and THE BLACK TARANTULA: when she and Peter moved to San Francisco, most new friends there called her "TBT." (She fit right in: one group of composers, associated with Robert Ashley and the Mills College Music Dept., where Peter was a grad student, lived in or near the "Honeymoon Hotel" in Berkeley: Clay Fear, Phil Harmonic, Rich Gold, and "Blue" Gene Tyranny.)

It wasn't only the slippery economic slope which suggested a literary cast to Kathy's existence: many events *were* truly larger than life. Most catastrophic was her mother's Christmas eve suicide: found dead of an overdose in a posh midtown hotel, after disappearing for days. The suicide greatly increased Kathy's considerable paranoia, and not just for obvious reasons. Prior to it, she had been hopeful about slightly better relations with her mother. They had achieved a recent rapprochement based on the odd circumstance of her mother becoming a Studio 54 habitué, and even running in circles where Kathy's "underground" literary reputation had some cachet.

Then, it was assumed her mother's suicide was due to finances; later, of course, it became impossible not to wonder about health problems. Kathy never learned her biological father's name: as far as she knew, her parents were never married. The utter distance she felt from the father with whom she grew up seemed to reflect her mother's feelings. Kathy was once approached by a distinguished looking gentleman who claimed that she was a member of the prominent New York Lehman family. (She was also related to the German-Jewish Ochs dynasty that owns the *New York Times*.)

Clearly, it's not easy to live out a myth, as children of the famous can testify. Many among them their most unique and accomplished ranks work diligently to keep away from, or sharply subdivide, their social and intellectual terrains from that of their parents. (Similarly, some political refugees I know with truly epic lives are resolute about normalizing daily routines, de-emphasizing and de-romanticizing their pasts.) In her *work*, Kathy was brilliantly in control of her own mythmaking tendency.

In an essay published in 1989 in *Review of Contemporary Fiction*, she discusses her current "post cynical" phase, in which "there's no more need to deconstruct, to take apart perceptual habits, to reveal the frauds on which our society's living. We now have to find somewhere to go, a belief...." She writes about her recently completed book, *Empire of the Senseless:*

> After having traveled through innumerable texts, written texts, texts of stories which people had told or shown me, texts found in myself, *Empire* ended with the hints of a possibility or beginning: the body, the actual flesh, almost wordless, romance, the beginning of a movement from no to yes, from nihilism to youth.

Her final novel, *Pussy, King of the Pirates*, is a wonderful fulfillment of this movement.

To me, it's an open question as to how confused Kathy herself was regarding being mythological Kathy, and how damaged by it. Certainly, as anyone who ever laid eyes on her knows, she constructed a striking, fetishistic image of herself, beginning with the earliest days of the Mudd Club. (She and its art curator, Diego Cortez, had collaborated on several performances prior to the opening.) In *Lust for Life: On the Writings of Kathy Acker*, Leslie Dick remembers sitting with Kathy at a party, "looking at her face, with its harsh makeup and amazing punk hair, peroxide blond then with brown burn marks on it...and recognizing this spectacle as a

mask that she peered out from behind, or within, oddly like a little girl."
She continues:

> her self-presentation (both live and photographic) through
> clothes, hair, exposure of skin, tattoos, etc., her presence
> on the covers of her books all worked explicitly to place
> her body as an obstacle, a threat and a promise, mediating
> between the reader and the text. Her small self-published
> books were like LPs, her readings were always a perfor-
> mance, and the sheer physical presence of her body and the
> sound of her voice were central to her project.

Kathy's reputation as occasional diva (to the max) was well deserved.
But that chiefly operated in a self-destructive manner, often alienat-
ing friends, rather than in customary obnoxious ways: she was a revered
teacher, for instance, and usually a courteous and personable customer. I
see these issues as aligned with Kathy's contempt for therapy (and deep fear
of mind control), which, of course, didn't prevent an exhaustive reading
of Freud and Lacan—she may have been one of three or four individuals
from Brandeis in the '60s who never went to a shrink!

All of this speaks to the heartbreaking, poignant questions (way beyond
my scope here) of why Kathy made the apparently irrational decision to not
have radiation following her mastectomy. And why, at that time, she had
recourse to virtually nobody with whom to discuss these decisions rationally.
(For one thing, she moved to London almost immediately after the surgery:
it seemed, in part, to avoid her friends bugging her about treatment.)

As to my personal history with Kathy, that would take volumes. We
were freshmen together at Brandeis, in the (itself mythic) class of '68.
Only nodding acquaintances there, we had several close mutual friends in
overlapping cliques of the "hip" students (at least a third of the school),
so I was privy to much gossip about her life. At an institution with sharp,
highly eccentric, original, and image-conscious students (I had grown a
beard the summer after high school to stake my claim), Kathy Alexander
stood out from the start. (Supposedly, the Ackers were represented in
Michael Weller's popular play *Moonchildren*, but she and I could never
identify them.)

One of a handful of classics majors, it was well-known that Kathy had entered proficient in Greek and Latin (which was astonishing to me, coming from the shitty public schools of Yonkers). Kathy seemed to live in the library, to study constantly, to devour books. Deeply intellectual, her look was vulnerable, pouty, experienced and sexy, somewhat androgynous. Kathy was involved with the very coolest upperclassmen, including several in Bob Acker's crowd who'd been in the historic big pot bust. The administration had told them to leave for a year and seek therapy (no doubt soul-searching was also recommended). On their return, they were required to live in the dorms—that's how I came to have a rapport with Bob, who was on my floor in his junior year.

Kathy was quite influential with the women in our class. Working independently, she and I were chief cheerleaders of D's gala weekend (she's now a professor at Harvard Law School) of losing her virginity—with a lanky, handsome (booted and side-burned) upperclassman who drove a motorcycle and played blues guitar. (I had somewhat of a crush on him: I was posing as "bi" then, which was chic, though being gay was still beyond the pale.) There was the memorable occasion when Kathy half-heartedly slit her wrists, and two other women on her floor immediately followed suit. The resident advisor (who later was rumored to have joined the Weather Underground) rushed into her room and insisted that Kathy stop immediately—otherwise, the whole dorm would be imitating her!

Kathy and I became close almost immediately in 1968, when I migrated from Brandeis to grad school at UCSD where she was finishing her undergrad degree. Caravanning out here with friends, including her freshman roommate, Tamar Diesendruck (a painter who later became a composer and won the Prix de Rome), four of us crashed on the Ackers' floor until we found a place to rent. Similar to students in Cambridge and environs, they were living in a spacious Victorian house with wood floors. Except, to find that in San Diego they had to travel to an old section near downtown—directly under the flight path at Lindbergh Field. That was over 15 miles away from the La Jolla campus which, like UC Santa Cruz, was designed during the Berkeley Free Speech Movement for maximum distance from any urban center. They hitched to school, or bummed rides. (Kathy never did learn to drive a car.)

Although by no means identifying as a hippie, Kathy baked bread, and sewed her own clothes (a marked contrast to Brandeis where she shoplifted them from trendy Design Research in Cambridge): perhaps an easier task than it sounds, since she wore the world's shortest skirts. Bob paced constantly. They played Chess and GO; we all played cards. (I remember a prolonged Bridge game on the floor with Kathy, at an anti-military research sit-in on campus.) Acker was quite impulse-ridden. The "Passover seder" they invited us to that first year consisted chiefly of him tying Tamar to a chair, which he sort of danced around maniacally, till Kathy, who usually appreciated Acker's less aggressive antics, made him desist. (I understand that he's now a corporate lawyer, and married to the [former?] best friend of the other woman from the original undergrad triangle: they met again at a class reunion; the ceremony was at the Taj Mahal.)

Primarily, then as always, Kathy was reading and writing. Working in virtual isolation, she was the first peer I knew well to take herself seriously as a writer. At that point, our few models here were from an older generation, like UCSD music professor Pauline Oliveros, and especially David Antin, critic and poet in the Visual Arts Dept. Kathy fervently "apprenticed" herself (as she called it) to David, auditing all of his classes. I followed, and we became fast friends with David and Eleanor, taking turns babysitting for their son, Blaise.

Both disgruntled with school, we had a Swift seminar together, where we annoyed everyone by incessantly passing notes and giggling. Highlights of our cultural life were the midnight, underground films at a theater way out in east San Diego (which soon turned to porn) that, amazingly, showed the likes of Brakhage and Kuchar. And the Anomaly Factory, a water tower on campus which a group of inspired undergrads, with the guidance of impresario David Cunningham, had turned into an innovative, computerized, high-tech theater-lab.

It was absolutely invaluable to witness Kathy's discipline and comprehensive structuring of her time for reading and writing, as well as self-confident experimentation and professional attitude about getting her work out. Although UCSD was new and in many ways vital (for a university), it was, and still is, rather easy for people in San Diego to behave as if they're on permanent vacation: many would-be dilettantes. Of course, what Kathy was writing *about* also became crucial to me, not to mention to postmodern thought—human identity, and how to get rid of (and/or retrieve) it! (Maybe the twins would heroically attempt both!)

Although we were the same age, Kathy always felt that she was a member of the younger generation of punks. (For one thing, she was considerably less seduced by psychedelic drugs; she did enjoy occasional coke or opium binges in the old days.) We shared a deep mistrust of utopian thinking: her chief, frequently reiterated, complaint against hippies. In "Blue Valentine," an essay for the British Film Institute's publication, *ANDY WARHOL: Film Factory*, she wrote: "People around me believed that they and hopefully all other people could and would only feel peace and love.... I felt isolated in this world, as if I was pitch black and everyone else, pastel." She went on to describe our mutual alienation in San Diego:

> I had one close friend, Melvyn Freilicher, still one of my dearest friends, who was also a literature graduate student and gay. I mention that he was gay because, at that time, just to become divorced was tantamount to expulsion from graduate school.... (Gay men, at best, were supposed to hide their love in the bathrooms.) For hours Melvyn and I would listen to Warhol's production of The Velvet Underground and fantasize about living in a society such as that of Warhol and his friends, a society in which the two of us weren't outcasts.

While being cynical about the possibilities of social harmony, I was less critical of hippies, but more concerned with the pernicious effect of utopian thinking on Marxist ideology of "scientific" history, and a Central Committee somehow inevitably spawning a classless society. An activist during Vietnam and afterwards, at the end of my stint, I worked mostly with artists organizations staging multi-media shows downtown, and attacking local "poverty program pimps" cum FBI agents. For 15 years, I also published *CRAWL OUT YOUR WINDOW*, a regional San Diego literary/arts magazine. (One pole of my Brandeis identity had been participating in many civil rights sit-ins, and anti-war marches.)

Kathy was extremely supportive of such organizing activities. Certainly, she shared the central axioms of our time concerning the pure and incorruptible evil of post-monopoly capitalism, and all governments which serve it—which is tantamount to saying that she breathed the same oxygen as the rest of us. Traveling frequently, wherever she went—Seattle, Minneapolis, East Berlin, London—Kathy investigated local scenes: meeting people running presses, alternative media, food coops, independent music labels, squatters rights groups. Our ongoing dialog on "alternative" cultures lasted a lifetime.

It's impossible to detail Kathy's significance to me. During my 20s, I was pretty much bicoastal, spending part of each year in New York. She introduced me to many artists and composers there (most notably, Rhys Chatham); some became boyfriends or hot sex. We both kind of avoided other writers, but were close to Jackson MacLow and Bernadette Mayer; Kathy used to take me over to Ted Berrigan's, I'd sometimes bring her to Ashbery's. She turned me onto writers way before anyone was discussing them, especially Bruno Schulz and Elias Canetti.

So many stellar individual events, like our wonderful Christmas eve dinner at (the mobbed) Second Avenue Deli. Afterwards, getting drunk at the Astor Hotel bar, where we composed telegrams to various men whom she wanted to entice and/or tell off; I'd go to the pay phone and send them. (We also wrote telegrams to the Antins and select others, requesting that they adopt us and be our family; those we didn't send.)

In terms of a sibling relationship, I was able to help Kathy in some concrete ways, in her numerous moves from city to city and coast to coast, or when she ran out of money to self-publish. As with virtually all of Kathy's close friends, many of our longest and most hilarious conversations over the years took place late at night, when she called in great pain over a boyfriend situation: relating what had transpired in vivid and obsessive detail. We'd laughingly envision remedial scenes, improvise dialogs and various types of merry retribution.

There's no simple way to describe, let alone deal with, the palpability of absence, which appears to be our chief Millennial legacy. Basically, for me, the short of it is this: life seems inconceivable without Kathy to properly narrate it. It seems, too, that it will always feel that way.

NOTE: *This piece was originally written soon after Kathy's death in 1997, and recently revised. Sadly, the final paragraph feels as true today as it did then.*

THE ENCYCLOPEDIA OF REBELS

1

While school was winding down in the spring, I started an excellent new cultural biography by David S. Reynolds, *JOHN BROWN, Abolitionist: The Man Who Killed Slavery, Sparked the Civil War, and Seeded Civil Rights*. Debunking the often prevailing sentiment that he was a paranoid lunatic, mostly promulgated in the Reconstruction era (which Reynolds sees as extending from 1870 to 1950!), John Brown is viewed as a pivotal figure: a Spartan, Cromwell-like Calvinist with rigidly egalitarian principles and experiences, brought up by strong anti-racist parents. (Another biographer commented that Brown "had a puritanical obsession with the wrongs of others.")

This was the most appealing in my huge pile of unread books, since John Brown appeared to react with appropriate urgency to his catastrophic era, which seems as dire as our own, only less repulsive to think about *because it isn't now*. As everyone on the left had predicted, Democrats winning the last Congressional elections had meant nothing in Iraq; the war "surges" away. Bush gangsters fervently destroying whatever world resources and peoples they couldn't manage to privatize (own).

The intelligentsia, at least, must have experienced similar levels of spiraling despair in the 1850s, after the Fugitive Slave Law passed, which greatly politicized Emerson, Thoreau and the Transcendentalists: among the first and loudest public voices calling for secession (though unlike John Brown, not known for putting their money where their mouths were), rightly viewing the country's capitalist machine as inextricably linked to the basest human exploitation.

Brown had lived and worked communally with several groups of black people in Ohio and New York, actively participated in the Underground Railroad, and was an important speaker and fundraiser though never a member of any organization. In Missouri, he liberated 11 slaves, killing a white man in the process, and led them on a precarious thousand-mile flight to freedom. In Springfield, Ohio, Brown founded an armed black cadre, The League of Gileadites, to fight the Fugitive Slave Law by attacking slave catchers. Moving to the Kansas territories in 1855, he reacted to the violent vigilantism between Free Staters and pro-slavery forces by further escalating the level of bloodshed which he believed crucial to ending slavery.

I had no idea how profoundly Kansas was then "in a state of war and near anarchy." Evidently, it was a common assumption, especially among Southerners, that Kansas was an all-or-nothing proposition: if it went for slavery, all the other territories would too. Reynolds succinctly characterizes its vigilante atmosphere which has been associated with the antebellum South: "eye-gouging, bowie-knife stabbing and scalping, hanging, burning over slow fires, whipping, tarring and feathering."

Not only were individuals on both sides kidnapped, ambushed and murdered in raids on their homes, but whole towns were attacked and sacked—Lawrence being a leading anti-slavery enclave, Leavenworth a pro-slavery center. Of the 52 individuals who died in Kansas slavery battles of 1855 to '58, almost 75 percent were Free State casualties. Only 8 pro-slavery advocates were murdered, 5 of them at the hands of John Brown's posse, including several of his sons, in his most controversial and vilified act: a retaliatory raid on the pro-slavery settlement of Pottawatomie.

Targeting politically active families, they broke into the Doyles' cabin, took the father and his two eldest sons into the woods where they "fell on them, hacking away with the heavy swords, and inflicting heavy wounds: Drury Doyle's finger and arms were severed, and his head and chest were gashed. His brother was stabbed through the head, jaw and side, and the father wounded in the breast." (After further assassinations that day, John Brown, Jr., at first exultant, became confused then deranged.) Soon afterwards, John Brown left the Kansas territories with plans well underway to seize the federal arsenal at Harper's Ferry, Virginia, and move against a large plantation to free as many slaves as possible, hoping that would spiral into a massive revolt.

Reynolds' descriptions of Kansas were beginning to sound like a low-tech Iraq: nobody was safe anywhere, and no neutral or mixed regions could be found. Even Native Americans, by far the largest ethnic group in the territories, living in communities which had newspapers and churches, held black slaves, especially the Cherokee farmers. And an "illiterate, coarse, slaveholding minister" had appropriated some of the Shawnee tribe's finest lands and erected a Shawnee Mission, a pro-slavery center.

Not surprisingly, the government aided pro-slavery forces: President Franklin Pierce appointed one of their own as territorial head. In 1854 and '55, ruffians from Missouri crossed into Kansas to stuff ballot boxes and elect a bogus legislature which passed stringent, but largely unenforceable black laws that made speaking against slavery a felony: two to five years of hard labor for anyone possessing an abolitionist publication, five years of hard labor for writers or publishers of anti-slavery texts, the death penalty for those who induced slaves to revolt.

Free Staters themselves were a wildly factionalized group. A large segment wasn't opposed to slavery but was promoting laissez-faire capitalism for white workers *only:* aiming to prevent all blacks, free or bonded, from living in the territories. Others were colonizationists who believed that blacks should be freed and sent back to Africa, because they saw no hope for equality here. Even after the Civil War, some abolitionists were adamant that blacks be made full and equal citizens while others maintained that each state should handle its own enfranchisement—*or not.*

Many Free Staters, along with moderate abolitionists, denounced interfering with slavery where it already existed. (When Lincoln first took office, he declared himself willing to sign a constitutional amendment to that effect.) A minority including Brown and his eastern financial backers,

"The Secret Six," increasingly shifted toward militancy, while mainstream leaders like William Lloyd Garrison continued advocating non-resistance, then "disunion"—after the North separated itself from the South, slavery would soon die out due to economic and social instability (echoes of Marx's equally improbable "withering away" of the state!).

At Harper's Ferry, Brown's band of 21, including 16 whites, quickly seized the arsenal, rifle factory, several bridges and local farms. Six liberators went five miles north to the farm of Colonel Lewis Washington, the great-grandnephew of George Washington, capturing this scion of the American Revolution at midnight, and forcing him to hand over to one of the black invaders, Osborne Anderson, the Lafayette pistol and the sword of Frederick the Great which were in his possession. Favoring symbolic gestures, Brown strapped on the sword in battle.

As in Pottawatomie, he attacked on Sunday, signifying his sacred mission. Earlier, while staying with Frederick Douglass, who admired Brown but tried to convince him of the unfeasibility of the Harper's Ferry scheme, Brown had convened a Constitutional Convention which drafted a new Constitution in direct response to the recent Dred Scott case in which the Supreme Court ruled that blacks couldn't bring lawsuits because they weren't citizens. (Soon after Brown was captured, federal agents were sent to arrest Douglass at his home in Rochester, but he'd fled to Canada, as had four members of "The Secret Six.")

When his initial successes at Harper's Ferry didn't provoke large-scale local slave uprisings, as he'd predicted—most of the "freed" slaves responded with indifference or fear—Brown became fatally indecisive. While praising him to the skies, Osborne Anderson who was also able to flee to Canada where he wrote his memoir, *A VOICE FROM HARPER'S FERRY*, comments that Brown's "tardiness" in considering a proposition for a prisoner exchange "was eventually cause of our defeat. It was no part of the original plan to hold on to the Ferry, or to parley with prisoners...."

Anderson goes on to condemn the slaveholders who neither honored the flag of truce, nor engaged in the fighting:

> Col. Washington, the representative of the old hero, stood "blubbering" like a great calf at supposed danger; while

the laboring white classes and non-slaveholders, with the
marines (mostly gentlemen from "furrin" parts,) were the
men who faced the bullets of John Brown and his men.
Hardly the skin of a slaveholder could be scratched in open
fight; the cowards kept out of the way until danger was
passed, sending the poor whites into the pitfalls....

Richard Realf, an officer in Brown's provisional government, reported
that Brown had greatly miscalculated the potential for cooperation
between black runaways and Native Americans. Having studied all the
books he could find on insurrectionary warfare, and focusing on Haiti,
Brown's schemes were influenced by the idea of fugitives staging surprise
attacks from inaccessible hideouts in the Virginia hills.

Throughout the Americas, many blacks *had* run away—quite a different affair than being "freed" by an unknown, wild-eyed, white man—and
lived in semi-permanent settlements, often with indigenous peoples; some
"maroon" colonies, especially in the Caribbean and Central America, lasted
for decades. From the mid 17th century to 1864, 50 such colonies arose in
this country, scattered in mountainous, forested or swampy areas—chiefly
the great Dismal Swamp in North Carolina and Virginia; Florida was
another site where Seminole Indians and blacks launched small but potent
guerilla battles during the Seminole Wars, costing the U.S. more than
$20,000,000, according to W.E.B. DuBois. (Viva Chief Osceola!)

Most of Brown's "army" quickly fled the Harper's Ferry area or were
killed (some gruesomely at the hands of the mob). At the end, Brown and
a few remaining men were holed up in an engine room, surrounded by an
intoxicated mob, and 12 state and federal militias commanded by Robert
E. Lee. The handsome actor John Wilkes Booth canceled a Richmond performance, and rushed to join the militia guarding the scaffold. But five
years later, in a letter he wrote to his sister, he appeared to revere Brown,
comparing him favorably to Lincoln, whom Booth saw as a kind of coarse
and vulgar Bonaparte. (When Lincoln's assassin was subsequently trapped
and killed in a barn near Bowling Green, Virginia, Booth's last reported
words were, "Useless, useless.")

In the several months prior to his execution with four of his men, Brown's eloquent speeches and writings gained widespread national attention. Emerson declared that John Brown "will make the gallows holy as the cross." In the final note he left right before his execution in Charlestown, Virginia in 1859, Brown wrote:

> I John Brown am now quite *certain* that the crimes of this *guilty, land will never be* purged *away; but with Blood.* I had *as I now think: vainly* flattered myself that without *very* much Bloodshed; it might be done.

Over 600,000 soldiers died in the Civil War over a four-year period, at a time when the total population of the United States was 35 million.

11

Gordon, an old friend, just went into the hospital, very *ill: he may finally succeed in drinking himself to death. Possibly coming home to die slowly, needing constant care which he can't afford, to not fall or burn down the house. Turns out he's had hepatitis C this whole time—he only told me his liver was damaged.*

Before that, Gordon had throat cancer, and continued to smoke cigarettes and pot while he was getting radiation. Three very close women friends were also being treated for cancer then—only one lived in town. All four had devoted partners, thank God, who I knew would see them through, though two of the couples had already talked about splitting up afterwards.

Eager to be helpful, I tried to stay in close contact, aware of their progress, fluctuations of treatment regimens: minimally, to just remain accessible. None was self-destructive like Gordon: certainly the only one with a crystal meth history. So far, post-chemo hell, the women are all doing well.

In the past, I needed to fix everything, somewhat as an activist for a decade or two, and especially with boyfriends: often (but not invariably) going straight for the addicted—alcoholics, druggies—or the artistes with "borderline" personalities fresh out of County Mental Health. All dead now.

Needing to be needed, much less pressing now: a lot of blood under that therapy bridge. (Joe, my longtime partner, and I were very involved in the daily lives of two wonderful, single friends who died of AIDS in the early '90s.)

Of course, I had always wanted someone to fix me...or just to pay more attention. (Hence the recurrent childhood fantasy that I was being scrutinized by unidentified observers over closed-circuit TV—à la the fabulous Burns and Allen show, though by no one nearly as benign.)

"Say goodnight, Gracie." ("Goodnight, Gracie.")

111

Reading about John Brown's last days coincided with getting Cindy Sheehan's Memorial Day email announcement that she was abandoning the peace movement. Reacting to the vitriolic criticism she'd been receiving ever since attacking the inert Democrats after their Congressional victories, Sheehan wrote that it was futile to try to "change a paradigm that is now, I am afraid, carved in immovable, unbendable and rigidly mendacious marble." Brown's officer, Richard Realf, had written a letter to Horace Greeley's progressive *Tribune* stating that John Brown and his followers had no faith whatsoever in the two party American political system, believing it had been utterly corrupted by slavery.

James Redpath, the Northern abolition leader, wrote in the *Liberator* that Brown had told him if the Republicans gained office, the American people would grow complacent, assuming slavery would disappear peacefully. About the two party system, Cindy Sheehan's statement flatly read: "If we don't find alternatives...our Representative Republic will die and be replaced with what we are rapidly descending into with nary a check or balance: a fascist corporate wasteland."

I remember when Clinton nominated Lani Guinier, a Harvard law school professor, as Assistant Attorney General, then withdrew the nomination two minutes after this articulate, mixed race Jewish/black woman started advocating on CNN for a multiple party, parliamentary system to help ensure minorities a reasonable chance of representation, rather than being subjected to the "tyranny of the majority," as James Madison had originally put it. Clinton claimed he had never read any of her publications; Guinier wasn't even allowed a public hearing.

A "heartbroken" Cindy Sheehan accused herself of naïve complicity, concluding that her son "did indeed die for nothing" in Iraq. Her email stated: "It is so painful to me to know that I bought into this system for so many years and Casey paid the price for that allegiance. I failed my boy and that hurts the most." Sheehan declared that because of her recent over-commitment to the anti-war movement, both her marriage and health had fallen apart, and her children become estranged.

However, returning from visiting my mother in Florida several months later, I saw Sheehan on CNN, in the Houston airport. The sound was off, but evidently she was intending to run against do-nothing liberal Speaker of the House, Nancy Pelosi, in the next election—hopefully to gain a lot of media attention. (Happily for us, it's probably too painful for Sheehan to sit still.)

Obviously, volumes could be written (by those with strong stomachs and hearty souls) about so many unsung and remarkable people right now who are reacting appropriately (i.e. extremely): including some of my colleagues from the New Left who haven't given up, as I apparently have, on trying to create social change. Just today, *San Diego CITYBEAT* had a cover story on Brad Will, an Indymedia video journalist who was killed by government agents in Oaxaca while reporting on police riots against the striking militant sector of the teachers' union. Workers had controlled parts of the city for a few weeks, setting up barricades in the streets, until the government sent in militia to mow them down. Knowing his life was in danger from the start, Will reportedly taped his own death. When arriving in Oaxaca with other foreign press, the radio was blaring, *"If you see a gringo with a camera, kill him!"*

Will had already covered Latin America extensively: filming the resistance of 12,000 squatters in a camp near the city of Goiania in Brazil when the military police swept in; riotous street protests against the Director of the InterAmerican Development Bank; interviews with Evo Morales before he was elected president of Bolivia. Prior to the World Trade Center towers collapsing and the social change movement in New York going into deep freeze, Will had documented the eviction of multiple squatters and community gardens as the city inexorably and brutally gentrified.

Apparently, a child of affluent parents—Brad Will could have had a cushy life.

1V

CONGRESSIONAL RE-DRESS: Wouldn't it be grand if Maxine Waters (D-CA) beat the shit out of Vice-President Dick ("non executive branch") Cheney in Congress! Echoing in reverse what happened on the floor of the Senate in 1856 when Charles Sumner, *the* leading anti-slavery Senator, was hammered almost to death with a gold-tipped, gutta percha cane, by the venerable Senator from South Carolina, Preston Brooks. Beat into unconsciousness, his blood flowed copiously on the Senate floor; Sumner suffered multiple lacerations on the scalp causing him to be out of the Senate for 3 years. (Brooks privately boasted that he had landed "about thirty first-rate stripes.")

Sumner had committed the unforgivable faux pas of insulting one of Brooks' relatives, also a Senator, by comparing him to Don Quixote!—blinded to reason by love for his mistress, his Dulcinea, "the harlot slavery." Testifying in the House hearings, Southern gentleman Brooks suggested that he'd evinced manly foresight by preventing himself from killing Sumner:

> it was expressly to avoid taking life that I used an ordinary cane, presented to me by a friend in Baltimore, nearly three months before its application to the "bare head" of the Massachusetts Senator. I went to work very deliberately, as I am charged and this is admitted and speculated somewhat as to whether I should employ a horsewhip or a cowhide, but knowing that the Senator was my superior in strength, it occurred to me that he might wrest it from my hand, and then for I never attempt anything I do not perform I might

have been compelled to do that which I would have regret-
ted the balance of my natural life.

Brooks resigned from the Senate, and was promptly reelected that same
year.

Sumner continued a distinguished career as the most prominent and
uncompromising elected advocate for African Americans' civil rights.
(Once when asked whether he ever looked at the other side of the slavery
question, Sumner replied: "There is no other side.") During the war, he
advocated the use of black troops. As Chairman of the Senate Committee on Foreign Relations, Sumner showed considerable skill in preventing
European intervention in the Civil War. Afterwards, he promoted univer-
sal suffrage for African Americans (opposing Lincoln who favored partial
enfranchisement), and the 1866 Civil Rights Bill which was designed to
protect freed slaves from extensive, restrictive Southern black codes.

Visiting Sumner at his home in Boston in 1857, John Brown asked to
see the coat the Senator was wearing when he'd been attacked. Still in pain
from the beating, Sumner hobbled to the closet and pulled out a rumpled,
bloodstained coat. Brown said nothing, but tightened his lips, and stared
at the coat, "as a devotee would contemplate the relic of a saint," one witness reported.

*As Samuel Adams allegedly remarked while plotting the Boston Tea Party,
they needed more than 3 or 4 people to die, in order to have martyrs—but
fewer than 10, because at that point it just became a sewage problem.*

V

*Two months before the presidential elections. McCain recently unleashed the
terrifyingly incompetent, rabid right wing Sarah Palin as his vice-presidential
running mate. A feisty gal who lots and lots of just plain folks would love to
have a beer with before (better yet, while) they enjoy machine gunning elk
and other large mammals from helicopters.*

It's already almost impossible (however tantalizing) to feel hope despite Obama's tremendously heartening nomination and popularity—with all the persistent racism that nobody's talking about; fears of his assassination are starting to appear redundant as we're simply being engulfed in waves of idiocy and greed.

Yesterday the stock market collapsed. (Hurricanes are destroying chunks of seaboards.)

"Drill, baby, drill"—the Republican Party's convention energy mantra; in other words, we've made sure there's no future, so juice it up, doll.

Hard to feel much beneath the hearty crust of anxiety. Is the "future" already a slack tautology?

1965, freshman year at Brandeis, my first sit-in: a weekend in the federal building in Boston during Selma, Alabama. At the end, we—my tribe: mostly I'd never seen these particular members before, and never would know them personally—were told to link arms and sing "We Shall Overcome," as the cops dragged us out. (Protect your heads.)

I believed those words: we had morality on our side, we'd inevitably win.

This is not *(exactly) a tale of Young Idealist Disillusioned (and oh so Hardened!), like many a superb French novel.*

I had already known something about the virulence of racism:

—Yonkers, where I grew, up was completely segregated—the downtown poor, the very poorest sections all black. In high school, I obtained a closer view when I started going to CORE meetings there (promising my parents I wouldn't sign anything).

—By junior high, I was in Manhattan with friends every chance I got (the saving grace: we could also get there on pubic transportation). The summer after my junior year, I had a job as a messenger in the city (not on a bicycle, and not on Wall Street). Largely pre-gentrified, stark economic and racial disparities were evident, and complex enough in some neighborhoods that you needed to have a map of the streets in your head: which ones were safe, mainly with families—which corners not to turn.

—*Like many kids, I assume, I was obsessed with watching the horrors of Little Rock school integration on TV, when I was 10.*

—*In college, I began tutoring right away in Roxbury, the black section of Boston, and soon came to realize how bitterly segregated that "cradle of liberty" city was.*

Nonetheless, I was 18 during Selma, and the feeling of righteous optimism was distinctly precious: so distant now. (Still easy enough to summon up the righteous part!)

My next civil rights sit-in later that semester was right out of a quintessential '60s movie. We spent a weekend on the sidewalk in front of the White House, under plastic sheeting: it was snowing—Huntley-Brinkley termed it a "slush-in." I can't remember what crisis we were responding to, or even how it felt under the plastic (though I can still visualize the scene).

On the chartered bus going back to school, I managed to sit next to Nick: virtually the only blond at Brandeis (practically tousle-headed), handsome, with a toothy grin, notoriously bisexual, and he played the lute!

Under the blankets, we moved toward each other; soon the groping commenced.

I was hugely excited—finally, after many years of unfulfilled pubescent desires. "I dreamt about this," I told Nick—meaning, fantasized.

I'd put my hand on his leg, and he'd place it on the bulging cock in his pants. I didn't know what to do with it, so back to his leg. We kept this up for the whole trip, except when I threw up out the window: having had more coffee that weekend than in all the rest of my life combined. (Guess they didn't know how else to keep us warm out there.)

As soon as we got to campus, we headed for Nick's dorm room. Turned out he did have an enormous cock, which I continued to not quite know what to do with. (My fantasies had never really extended much beyond adoration, into the realm of action.) We had sex while Richard, who'd been after both of us, pounded and pounded on the door.

But Richard hadn't gone to the sit-in.

V1

Leon Harris opens his serviceable 1975 Upton Sinclair biography with a quote: *"We never had but one room at a time, and I slept on a sofa or cross-ways at the foot of my parents' bed.... One adventure recurred; the gas-light would be turned on in the middle of the night, and I would start up, rubbing my eyes, and join in the exciting chase of bedbugs. They came out in the dark, and went scurrying into hiding when they saw the light; so they must be mashed quickly."*

"These flat, reddish-brown, stinking bedbugs, along with the other many obscenities of poverty, explain why Upton Sinclair became a rebel," declares Harris. "What made his childhood experiences with poverty far worse than they would have been had he known nothing else was his constant moving back and forth between wretched boardinghouses and then homes of rich relatives." Yet experiencing the unhappiness of those relatives up close, Harris suggests, helped orient Sinclair toward socialism, deterring him from seeking affluence.

The etiology of rebels is doubtless too complex and fruitless a topic for our sketchy sketches. Still, the young Upton clearly did react against his father, a hopeless drunk, by developing a puritanical and abstemious personality which kept him away from booze, sex (to the despair of his first wife), and many foods (he wrote several books on fasting and raw food regimens). His *The Cup of Fury,* penned by "one who had but three or four sips of liquor" in his whole life, is all about writers and artists who had allegedly been destroyed by alcohol: among others, Jack London, Sinclair Lewis, Dylan Thomas, O. Henry, Stephen Crane, Isadora Duncan, Edna St. Vincent Millay, Hart Crane.

While these individuals "have set the intellectual and moral tone of our time...in the end the examples they give us is of sickness of mind and soul," Sinclair contends. "They have helped bring about an America in which people feel they 'must' drink." He claims that Sherwood Anderson's death, on a liner bound for Brazil, from abdominal congestion and peritonitis was a kind of collateral damage: result of swallowing the toothpick in a "cocktail-sausage" at the farewell party given him in the ship's stateroom.

After the huge success of *The Jungle* in 1906, Sinclair's exposé of the meatpacking industry which made him well respected, particularly by European leftists, he turned out many hastily written books and articles that, generally, didn't sell well, and he became known as a crank with a genius for self-promotion (although his prolonged campaign to be awarded the Nobel Prize was unsuccessful). But Sinclair always claimed to be promoting socialism, not himself, especially when he was almost elected governor of California in 1934 on the Democratic Party ticket (after running several times as a socialist) in the middle of the Depression, despite a vicious, red-baiting media campaign against him led by the ultraconservative *LA Times* owner, Harry Chandler, William Randolph Hearst (who was summoned from his vacation with a Nazi agent, "Huffy" Hanfstaeng; they had flown to Germany to interview Hitler), and pre-eminently by Hollywood mogul, Louis B. Mayer's fake ***NEWSREELS***:

> **Interviewer** (small): For whom are you voting, "comrade?"
>
> **Suspicious Person** (swarthy, bad teeth): Vy, I am foting for Seenclair.
>
> **Interviewer:** Why on earth are you voting for Mr. Sinclair?
>
> **SP:** Vell, his system worked vell in Russia, vy can't it work here?

Sinclair's EPIC (End Poverty in California) gubernatorial campaign called for establishing a network of cooperative colonies for the state's 700,000 unemployed. The rural economy had been the scene of bloody clashes between migrant laborers and management, culminating in a series of strikes involving thousands of workers; vigilante teams roamed the San Joaquin and Imperial Valleys, smashing all signs of union activity. EPIC's program entailed seizing idle factories and vacant farmland: the state would then capitalize and manage these cooperatives which would exchange their products within a giant, cash-free network. Modeled, though Sinclair didn't say so, on Soviet collective farms, they were to be seedbeds of a radical new "production for use" rather than for profit economy.

Sinclair was also responsible for converting the divine Charlie Chaplin to socialism before he was thrown out of the country for making too many people laugh. (When Sinclair got involved in mental telepathy experiments, he invited Chaplin and Theodore Dreiser to séances at his home, where a drunken Dreiser would fall asleep.) Critics viewed only two of Sinclair's subsequent novels as well written: *Oil* and *Boston*. *Boston* concerned the Sacco–Vanzetti case (about which Sinclair's biographer comments, "Not since the conviction of John Brown had a court's decision about a previously unknown individual so stirred Americans on both sides of the issue").

Throughout the trials and executions, Sinclair remained their staunch and important public advocate, but later research brought him to the disquieting conclusion, roundly rejected on the left, that at least Sacco was probably guilty of the holdup of a shoe factory and murder of a paymaster and his guard, and Vanzetti knew about that. The truth is impossible to ascertain. The unscrupulous prosecuting lawyer had coached and badgered witnesses, withheld exculpatory evidence, and perhaps tampered with physical evidence. The hostile judge made remarks during the trial like, "Did you see what I did with those anarchistic bastards the other day? I guess that will hold them for awhile."

Sacco and Vanzetti both had substantial alibis, and neither had ever been arrested; but they *were* militant anarchists, followers of Luigi Galleani, publisher of *Cronaca Sovversiva (Subversive Chronicle)*, an "Anarchist Weekly of Revolutionary Propaganda" which preached insurrectionary violence and armed retaliation, including the use of dynamite and assassination. (The 1917 Sedition Act made subscribing to that specific paper mandatory grounds for deportation.)

Italian anarchists had settled in every part of the United States: working in the garment and construction industries in New York, as operatives in the great silk factories of Paterson, quarry workers of Boston, cigar makers of Philadelphia and Tampa; and in many states as barbers, machinists, tailors and bricklayers. Generally, they espoused direct action, and did not play a conspicuous role in the American labor movement: becoming visible chiefly to support strikes as a means to reveal the blatant cruelty and contradictions of capitalism.

CHAIRMAN MAO COMES TO SAN DIEGO

The year, 1972. The setting: a household of lesbian Maoists, dressing to go to a cell meeting. Off come combat boots, jeans, flannel shirts. On go bras, stockings, garters, dresses; hair is teased, makeup and perfume carefully, if inexpertly, applied. Looking like female impersonators, they leave. Mel and his friend, Toni, the one roommate who didn't drop out of grad school at UCSD to go work in a factory, have been sitting on the bed watching.

> **Mel:** Who do they think they're kidding?
>
> **Toni:** Well, the central committee is like your parents—it's okay as long as you don't show it or talk about it.
>
> **Mel:** Gay is Bourgeois Decadence, I know. That's so fucked up. They're lucky they don't have to dress like that at work.
>
> **Toni:** Oh, Cait's not at NAASCO anymore.
>
> **Mel:** I like Cait a lot—she's the only one of them who's actually working class.
>
> **Toni:** She just got a job at a power plant, on the night shift.
>
> **Mel:** Really? I didn't think she was a "night person."
>
> **Toni:** She's not. It's so she can shut it down.
>
> **Mel:** What?!
>
> **Toni:** "When the call comes."
>
> **Mel:** Oy!
>
> **Toni:** Heresy in this household, I know—but at least the Trots acknowledge gays as an "oppressed minority."
>
> **Mel:** Yeah, and look what happened to Trotsky!

Not long afterwards, that house became important as the informal head-quarters of the NAASCO 7 Defense Committee: other former grad students we knew who worked in the shipbuilding yard, including a much-liked Chicano couple, had gained minor media attention by calling a wildcat strike to protest perilous health and safety conditions. Two days later, an explosion at NAASCO killed several workers; suddenly, these prescient, maverick unionists were all over the local news: turn on the TV, see a secret Commie!

Soon, an undercover agent convinced them to buy various firearms, and, if I remember correctly, they were arrested coming back in their van, in a sting operation broadcast live. Although we kept asking ourselves how they could have made such a dumb move, the answer was obvious. Agent provocateurs were masters at manipulating party members, using a line that confirmed their deepest fears and heartfelt beliefs: fascism is just around the corner—revolution now or never.

For most of us here in the heart of the military machine, "revolution" just sounded like the wish to live in Berkeley! Fascism, however, did have a certain ring of conviction.

Most scholars basically view Martha Canary, a.k.a. Calamity Jane, as a drunken prostitute. Leaving Missouri with her family around 1865, Martha was orphaned by the time she reached the Dakotas and Wyoming. She worked on and off as a prostitute, cook, laundress, dance hall girl, scout, and allegedly a horse rustler who also cut down cedar logs to sell to ranchers; she did ride into Deadwood with Wild Bill Hickok, but they weren't intimates.

Martha often wore men's clothes, though that was illegal in some areas: testimonies indicate that her "habits were thoroughly masculine, and that she frequently danced with the girls just as the men did." At different times, Martha ran several dance halls; one tale has her as co-proprietor with Madame Bull Dog who the *Montana State Guidebook* claimed "tipped the scales at 190, stripped. And stripped she was most of the time." Once, when they quarreled, "Madame Bull Dog tossed Calamity Jane into the street 'as easy as licking three men.'" Martha did not fight back: "Calamity was tougher 'n hell, but she wasn't crazy."

Another story had her running a brothel with Madame Moustache in Montana. There's an account of the summer of 1876 in Deadwood, when only three women (all with fantastic names like Big Dollie, Tid Bit, Dirty Em, Smooth Bore, and Sizzling Kate) were available for saloon hall dancing. So a man "was dressed in feminine garb, corseted and padded with closely shingled hair," and sold liquor as easily as the women.

Later, Calamity Jane helped turn herself into a mythological figure by touring with popular Wild West shows, playing herself, and writing a fallacious autobiography in which she was a lover of Wild Bill Hickok, frontier scout, stagecoach and pony express driver, and had an important role in General George Crook's campaign against the Sioux Indians. Her actual life is somewhat obscured by multiple rumors, partly because there were a number of other Calamity Janes to whom various legends accrued.

Calamity Jane was the heroine of more than half of Edward Wheeler's 33 extremely popular dime novels in the *Deadwood Dick* series, sequential in plot like soap operas. Her biographer, James D. McLaird, claims that such legendary feats as battling Cattymount Cass, or being kidnapped by Tra-la-la- Charlie, did *not* become part of the folklore, but he suggests that Martha's status as a dime novel heroine added to the willingness of listeners to accept her own tales as fact.

Wheeler, whose letterhead stated his avocation as "Sensational novelist," depicted Jane as beautiful, a force for the good. While he allowed her some latitude to violate society's codes—she's an excellent shot, outstanding rider, dresses like a man, and occasionally smokes cigars—she also wears diamond rings, a massive gold chain, and "slippers of dainty pattern upon the feet"; her blouse, when open at the throat, partially reveals a "breast of alabaster purity." After Deadwood Dick kisses Jane, she quickly returns to traditional submissiveness, awaiting "the appointed time when she should go to claim the love and protection of the only man she ever worshipped."

V11

Both of John Brown's parents came from families filled with Calvinistic piety. His father, Owen Brown, was a farmer and cobbler whose roots probably went back to the Mayflower. John's grandfather died in the Continental Army camp in New York when his son Owen was five; he and his 10 siblings were partly raised by religious relatives where he was exposed to anti-slavery sermons of Jonathan Edwards, Jr. Owen Brown was an abolitionist, and reliable conductor on the Underground Railroad; his son grew up with those attitudes—unlike most of his contemporaries, John never had a conversion experience to abolitionism. Reynolds claims that Brown's attitudes toward slaves were free of the condescension and snobbery which characterized many of even the most zealous abolitionists like Sumner who were born into the east coast establishment.

As a father himself, John Brown, disciple of Edwards' stern doomsday sermons, believed that his own sins were reflected in his children's disobedience (he had 20 of them, mostly with one wife; 7 sons and 4 daughters lived to maturity). Brown kept a ledger of John Jr.'s offenses which he often showed the boy:

—For disobeying mother…8 lashes
—For unfaithfulness at work…3 lashes

Finally, when Brown, a failed entrepreneur and businessman, decided the boy's "debits" outnumbered his "credits," he took his son into the barn for an "accounting": seizing a beech switch, he gave the boy a third of his apportioned lashes. Then stopping unexpectedly, Brown took off his own shirt and bent down, commanding his son to whip him. The father cried, "Harder, harder, harder!" until blood bubbled on his back, and he had "received the balance of the account."

Dalton Trumbo's father was an unsuccessful beekeeper and grocer, his mother a convert to Christian Science (like Daniel Ellsberg's), and daughter of a sheriff. Dalton's father had quietly opposed prejudice. During WW1, Orus Trumbo first resigned as secretary, then quit altogether, the semi-secret Loyalty League in Grand Junction, Colorado, when it started colluding with anti-German American vigilante activities. In one case, a German tailor had his shop ransacked; even the cloth from his ironing board was stripped off as they allegedly looked for secret documents from the Kaiser. In another, a German farmer was tarred and feathered.

After the war, further disillusionment led to Trumbo writing the acclaimed anti-war novel *Johnny Got His Gun*. Working in a bookstore in Grand Junction whose owner, a young veteran, had returned blind from France, it was one of Dalton's tasks to call for him each morning; he would meet Dalton in dark glasses. When they arrived at work, Dalton would heat a pan of water and drop in the blind veteran's glass eyes: the winter cold was so intense that if they had been put in without first being warmed, they would have frozen in the sockets.

Trumbo grew up determined to both write novels and make money. As a young man, he rapidly became a successful B script writer: going from reader to screenwriter at Warner Brothers, his salary skyrocketed from $35 to $100 in one week. (Before that, he produced six unpublished novels while working in a bakery which fed the local police who were running a nearby prostitution ring.) As one of the Hollywood Ten, Trumbo spent 11 months in federal prison for refusing to answer the House Un-American Activities Committee's questions in 1947 concerning membership in the leftist Screen Writers Guild (he'd been president for awhile), and the Communist Party.

> Spartacus is stabbed then decapitated by many smug dictators; somehow, somewhere, someone doesn't puke.
>
> **All** (in unison, with utmost sincerity): He wasn't a god, he was a simple man, a slave, I loved him.

Originally joining the CP in 1943, Trumbo briefly rejoined in 1955, right in the middle of the blacklist period, as a protest. He also refused studio heads' repeated injunctions to resign from the Guild, and align with the industry-controlled Screen Playwrights instead. Of course, like many of the blacklisted writers, Trumbo continued working in Hollywood, using fronts' names, until he was finally given credit again in 1960 for writing two blockbusters, *Spartacus* and *Exodus*: paving the way for the rehabilitation of some of the other directors, writers, and actors who hadn't already killed themselves.

About a year after the bust (the NAASCO 7 eventually got off on probation), a leftie hospital worker spotted the suspected agent provocateur; his wife was having a baby—registered under a different name than the one he'd been using; let us say "Bill King." Several local underground papers did some research, including the *San Diego Street Journal* whose considerable successes in the past were instrumental in putting one of Nixon's chief financial henchmen, C. Arnholt Smith, in prison, and could be measured in direct proportion to how frequently their offices, and sometimes homes, were firebombed.

That paper had been co-founded by Lowell Bergman, a grad student at UCSD, studying with radical Marxist philosopher, and New Left icon, Herbert Marcuse; later in his career, Bergman broke the tobacco industry cover up on Mike Wallace's show.

Fascinating and repugnant, San Diego was truly the wild west then. Leftist groups were frequently called upon to put our bodies on the line at WomanCare, the only abortion provider in town, as I recall, till it merged with Planned Parenthood. At different points, Marcuse was getting so many death threats that some of his grad students took turns sleeping at his house—armed.

The paper published Bill King's photo and aliases as part of their baseball card series of the local Red Squad: GET THE WHOLE SET, TRADE THEM WITH YOUR FRIENDS! With long, unkempt, curly dark hair, thick beard, customary Army jacket, and strident voice, King might have been a disgruntled vet (not a college student).

A few years later, he inadvertently came to play an odd but key role in my own arts organizing strategies. That followed my involvement with a Farm Workers support group which raised money, and picketed Safeways on weekends during the seemingly endless grape boycott.

Keeping a designated number of feet away from the entrance, trying to convince shoppers not to go inside, upped my alienation from San Diego by several substantial notches: unionists and their sympathizers left imme-

diately; most others were oblivious or hostile. By the end of my rather prolonged participation, I much preferred standing by the roadside for hours
holding a sign over having to speak.

The breaking point came when a group of hippies merrily skipped out
of the store one day, and offered us some trail mix.

"Don't eat it," I shrieked, "it might be poisoned!"

It was then I realized I couldn't do this anymore; I had to be more
involved with my own community, which I was increasingly eager to define
outside (but not exclusively) the schools and the gay scene.

VIII

Perhaps the most revelatory and grimly heartening sections of Reynolds'
book were tales of brave, hard-line and little known, white abolitionists
who lived and died for the cause decades before the Civil War, especially in
the period following Nat Turner's 1831 rebellion. When Brown wanted to
stir militancy in the all black League of Gileadites, he declared, "Have any
of you seen the Branded Hand? Do you remember the names of Lovejoy
and Torrey?"

In November, 1837, the murder of Illinois anti-slavery editor Elijah P.
Lovejoy mobilized key figures like Wendell Phillips into the abolitionist
movement, and turned Brown away from pacifism. In St. Louis, a mob
had destroyed the press in his office after Lovejoy editorialized against the
lynching of a black, and had moved across the Mississippi River to Alton,
Illinois where he repelled several assaults on his paper, with his rifle, though
the press was thrown into the river three times.

Faced with the suspension of his newspaper at a town meeting, Lovejoy
boldly defended his right to free speech. Soon afterwards, a furious mob
of pro-slavery citizens overpowered twenty guards who had been assigned
to protect his printing press. In the melee, Lovejoy was fatally wounded.
Lincoln called this the "most single important event that ever happened
in the new world."

DENMARK VESEY

MOTHER JONES

UPTON SINCLAIR

REV. CHARLES T. TORREY

DR. MARIE EQUI

BILL HAYWOOD

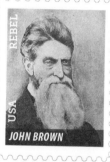

JOHN BROWN

AARON DWIGHT STEVENS

JANE ADDAMS

DALTON TRUMBO

GERONIMO PRATT

SACCO & VANZETTI

The Reverend Charles T. Torrey was a Yale educated Congregational minister who held pastorates in New Jersey and Massachusetts before giving up the ministry to move to Maryland. In December, 1841, he went to Washington as a newspaper correspondent and suffered a brief detention in jail for attending a slaveholders convention in Annapolis as a reporter. From his residence in Baltimore, he assisted in the escape of nearly 400 slaves (according to the "Yale Slavery & Abolition" website).

Finally, given 6 years of hard labor for slave stealing, Torrey received indications that he could be released from jail if he admitted to committing a crime. He refused, asserting, "I cannot afford to concede any truth or principle to get out of prison." Torrey died of tuberculosis there at age thirty-three. His body was taken to Boston for internment, where his memorial service attracted a huge crowd.

Reynolds declares that no slave rescuers were as militant as Lysander Spooner, a lawyer and anarchist who argued against Garrison, claiming that the Constitution did not embrace slavery, and since it was illegal and immoral, blacks had the right to bear arms. He published a kind of "how to" revolt pamphlet (apparent precursor to the 1971 *Anarchist's Cookbook*) that Brown tried to suppress, viewing it as counter-productive to his Harper's Ferry scheme (which Spooner, in turn, opposed as premature).

I was glad to discover that a Jew from Vienna, August Bondi, was one of Brown's Kansas fighters. (The "Jewish Virtual Library" features a funny story about Bondi and 2 friends shouting back and forth in Yiddish on the front lines.) As a teenager, Bondi fought under Louis Kossuth during the Hungarian war for liberty against Austria; he and his family were exiled.

In Kansas, Bondi was terrorized by pro-slavery men from Missouri who burned his house and trading post, and stole his horses and cows, while federal troops looked on. But having witnessed extreme brutality on slave ships, he was determined to stay in Kansas as part of the Free State forces. Later, Bondi became a land clerk, postmaster, local court judge, school board member, director of state charities and trustee of the Kansas Historical Society.

One of the few women mentioned in Reynolds' book, Prudence Crandall, a Quaker, also found refuge in Kansas where her abolition work was later officially recognized. After being boycotted for admitting one black pupil to an all girls school, in 1833 Crandall opened an establishment for "Young ladies and Misses of colour" in Connecticut which attracted girls from all over the eastern seaboard. Connecticut invoked a vagrancy law against these students who could be given 10 lashes of the long whip, then passed a "Black law" prohibiting the education of black children from out of state.

Jailed briefly, Crandall won her case, but several fires forced her to close the school within 2 years. Over a hundred years later, legal arguments used in Crandall's 1834 trial were submitted to the Supreme Court as part of the Brown v. Topeka Board of Education desegregation case.

IX

As soon as school's over in a few weeks, I need to pick up momentum for writing, and pursue some tantalizing gay intimations in John Brown's circle. Before blessed summer ends, and I become engulfed again in the fifth circle of paper grading hell, I also want to delve into my pile of Mother Jones, Wobblies and American labor history books with at least a bit of the attention those heroic individuals deserve. I hardly know anything about Kate Richards O'Hare, for instance, or Mother Bloor, whose very name makes me salivate with anticipation—except I just read that she was on the Central Committee of the American Communist Party in the '20s.

It feels strange to not be focusing on American black leaders, as usual: already read, and written, about Bayard Rustin, A. Philip Randolph, and Malcolm X. But what about the Fannie Lou Hamer bio I recently picked up, along with the writings of celebrated Caribbean Marxist C.L. R. James? Realistically, I won't get to the Europeans till next summer either—alas, Rosa Luxemburg!—or to wonderful Dorothea Day.

GOOGLING Elizabeth Gurley Flynn, I unexpectedly came across the fantastic story of Dr. Marie Equi, a new lesbian heroine. Flynn had lived with Equi for the last eight years of her life after she'd nursed Flynn back to health from a heart attack while on a west coast speaking tour on behalf of Sacco and Vanzetti. Before recent feminist scholarship, Marie Equi was primarily known as the physician who was arrested with Margaret Sanger in 1916, and sentenced to San Quentin prison in 1920 for three years (later commuted to one-and-a-half) for her anti-war views. (Her appeal was handled by C.E.S. Wood, a friend of Clarence Darrow: the state of Oregon's *Blue Book* refers to him as the most colorful figure in Oregon history.)

Equi lived in a "Boston marriage" in Oregon in 1893 with Bess Holcomb, a schoolteacher she met at Wellesley College. When Bess was short-changed $100 by her employer, Marie Equi flogged him with a rawhide whip in public: after calling Rev. Orson D. Taylor out of his realtor's office, and waiting for several hours, she went inside, began lashing him, and kicking and biting when he tried to restrain her. (Barbara Stanwyck, move over!) The local papers were snide, the townspeople sympathetic: more so several days later when Rev. Taylor was indicted by a Portland grand jury on charges of embezzling from dozens of local investors in a shady real estate scheme.

The couple moved to San Francisco where Marie continued her studies, returning to Portland to be one of the first female graduates of the University of Oregon Medical School. For organizing a team of nurses and physicians that traveled to San Francisco in 1906 to help earthquake victims, Equi was given a special commendation by the U.S. Army. That year she met her lifelong companion, Harriet Speckart, niece of the Olympia Brewing Co. founder, who began as Equi's assistant; Dr. Equi was one of only a handful of doctors in Portland at that time who would perform abortions.

Equi's commitment to the struggles of working women intensified in 1913 when she joined the picket line at the Oregon Packing Company, aided by the Wobblies. The police brutalized the striking women cherry pickers, including Dr. Equi whom they also arrested when she was trying to assist one of the workers. From that point on, she espoused anarchy and the destruction of capitalism, and became a revered member of the IWW (though, owing to her profession, not a dues paying one).

In 1916, Equi joined the American Union Against Militarism, and participated in a huge, pre-war protest rally in downtown Portland, unfurling a large banner, reading: PREPARE TO DIE, WORKINGMEN, J.P. MORGAN & CO. WANT PREPAREDNESS FOR PROFIT." The banner was torn from her hands, and she was forced to kiss the flag. Found guilty under a newly amended Sedition Act, Dr. Equi was monitored for the rest of her life by the Dept. of Justice. At her trial, an agent called her a "damn anarchist, a degenerate, and an abortionist."

The Corvallis Community Pages website offers tantalizing glimpses of a complex personal life: they adopted an infant girl (Harriet was "ma" and Equi was "da") who at sixteen was the youngest woman ever to fly an airplane solo in the Pacific Northwest. In the middle of their relationship, Harriet married an IWW organizer for two months. During her incarceration, in correspondence with friends, Equi questioned her own "queerness." Some friends thought Marie was in love with the bisexual Margaret Sanger who wrote about Marie: "To me she was like a crushed falcon which had braved the storm and winds of time and needed tenderness and love. I liked Marie always."

GUNS AND (SELF-)CONTROL, IN WEST PALM BEACH

2008: My brother, David, from New York, and I are visiting my mother: we're meeting my cousin L, and her husband, B, for dinner at their favorite expensive restaurant, smugly crowning a tall office building. Each table is pushed against the floor to ceiling windows, with sweeping vistas of the inland waterway and glistening ocean beyond. The inside is dim enough to exude ersatz elegance.

In the elevator, my mother, whom I recently turned on to her favorite show, Rachel Maddow, admonishes us for the nth time not to talk politics. (Poor kids from Brooklyn who never went to college, my cousins now own a lot of real estate.) I have every reason to placate them: they're my mother's only relatives in Florida, and they're very kind to her.

In the restaurant, L and B are already drunk. B is ostentatiously flirting with all of the waitresses by name. We are seated.

B (hearty): Did I ever show you guys my gun collection?

Mel and brother Dave exchange quick glances.

Mel: No.

B: Remind me to show it to you sometime. It's extensive. I just got a musket from the Civil War.

SILENCE.

Dave (conversationally)**:** What's your most expensive gun?

B: Probably the musket.

SILENCE.

L: Of course, they're not loaded…except for that one you keep near the bed in the safe.

Cousin L takes something out of her purse, and cockily tosses it across the table. It's her special permit to carry a concealed weapon. (I feel grateful that she hasn't thrown the weapon. To be fair, L *is* a realtor, which could conceivably place her in dicey situations.)

B (to Mel, who lives in the meth capital of the universe)**:** Believe me, if you lived in Florida, you'd have a gun within 6 months.

SILENCE.

Mel (in a neutral tone)**:** Have you ever been robbed?

L: No. But we *never* go west of the I-95.

Recognizing a (very) thinly veiled racist comment, Mel quickly tries to change the subject to the abject state of California's economy.

B: I bet Sarah Palin would make a better governor than the Terminator.

Mel and Dave exchange more quick glances.

Mel: Really? She couldn't even name one newspaper she read. She just said "all of them…."

Mother flashes a warning glance.

L: She's a doer, not a…!

SILENCE.

Mel fills in: not an effete intellectual like you!

L: And she wouldn't destroy *our* health care with socialized medicine.

SILENCE.

Dave: So, *where* do you keep your guns?

X

Plunging gaily onward, I observed that whoever had compiled the "Conspirators Biography" website, citing multiple sources, including two contemporaneous bios of John Brown, seemed to be titillated by the homoerotic, and keenly attentive to the physical attributes of Brown's "army": John Henry Kagi was "cold in manner, rather coarse of fiber and rough in appearance" (and an agnostic to boot!), and Charles Plummer Tidd "was by no means handsome" (however, he was kind-hearted).

On the other hand, Albert Hazlitt was "a good-sized, fine-looking fellow, overflowing with good nature and social feelings" while Dauphin Thompson was "very quiet, with fair, thoughtful face, curly blonde hair, and baby blue eyes," and although of a rather wild disposition, Mrs. Annie Brown Adams found William Leeman "very hand-some and very attractive."

Most provocative was the figure of Aaron Dwight Stevens, a militant compatriot who was executed with Brown. Great-grandson of a captain in the Revolutionary Army, Stevens had served in the Mexican War: convicted of mutiny, engaging in a drunken riot, and assaulting an officer, his life sentence was commuted to three years hard labor by President Franklin Pierce. Escaping from military prison, Stevens joined the Kansas Free State forces. A "man of superb bravery and of wonderful physique, he was well over six feet, was blessed with a great sense of humor"—*and* he never married!

A spiritualist who engaged in séances, Stevens often led this cadre in discussions of Thomas Paine's infamous critique of organized religion, *The Age of Reason*. Brown's legal counsel at Harper's Ferry was apparently rather hot for the seriously wounded Stevens: "He bears his sufferings with grim and silent fortitude...he is a splendid looking young fellow. Such black and penetrating eyes! Such an expansive brow! Such a grand chest and limbs!" In *To Purge This Land with Blood,* Stephen Oates describes Stevens as "a tall, hulking man with an explosive temper and black brooding eyes." I was somewhat disappointed to discover that he wrote love letters to Jennie Dunbar in West Andover, Ohio. But this 1984 Brown biography did put me onto another exciting, if far less hunky, gay track: Thomas Wentworth Higginson—famed Emily Dickinson correspondent. One of the "Inner Four," the most committed of Brown's eastern financial backers, in 1854, Higginson played a key role in the residents of Worcester, Mass. launching a crusade against the Fugitive Slave Law. When a mob broke into the Boston courthouse, he smashed in the jailhouse door, attempting to liberate Anthony Burns, a very popular runaway who could be returned to his captors only by calling in the federal militia.

First meeting Brown in 1857, after a tour of the smoldering Kansas countryside, Higginson was organizing a disunion conference in Worcester where he was a Unitarian minister at the Free Church, preaching to "radicals of all descriptions." Having urged Brown not to postpone the Harper's Ferry raid, afterwards Higginson and Lysander Spooner tried organizing an escape plan, against Brown's wishes. During the Civil War, Higginson went on to command an all-black volunteer unit from South Carolina.

As a shy and introspective youth who entered Harvard at 13, Higginson befriended another future "Secret Six" member, Theodore Parker. A physical fitness buff, Higginson ran everywhere, did calisthenics, and played something like touch football. Teaching for awhile in Samuel Weld's school for boys, he then felt called upon to preach, and entered Harvard's Divinity School where he formed a "romantic attachment" with a "brilliant youth" named William Hulbert whom he loved "out of the depths of my heart."

Supposedly, Higginson became bored with the school's curriculum, and was a recluse for awhile before plunging into abolitionist politics, and working with the Underground Railroad. This illuminating bio informs us that he married Mary Elizabeth Channing, "a highly intellectual but sickly woman who was an invalid during most of their married life" (his second cousin, according to another source). However, "in his zealous work he still found time to write loving letters to his friend Hulbert, as was the custom among male friends in the Victorian era."

In his groundbreaking 1976 tome, *GAY AMERICAN HISTORY*, Jonathan Katz discusses Higginson's complex sexuality, contending that the 19th century model of non-sexual male friendship, and "the existence of only a heterosexual model for conceptualizing sexual feelings" allowed him and others (including Thoreau) to openly express their passions for friends. Higginson wrote to his mother that "slender, graceful," black-eyed, "raven" haired Hulbert is "like some fascinating girl."

In 1914, Higginson's widow wrote innocently of her late husband's "romantic friendship" with Hulbert as being "more like those between man and woman than between two men." Apparently Higginson balanced these feelings *(how happily?)* and his concern with physical fitness and masculinity with an advocacy of woman's emancipation, and a minister's deep, puritanical concept of sin, evident in his venomous attacks on the "Unmanly Manhood" of Walt Whitman and Oscar Wilde.

Often needing to re-explain to myself the prominence of such hateful gay men as J. Edgar Hoover, Roy Cohn and their ilk, I invoke W.E.B. Dubois' "double consciousness," and Paulo Freire's notion of the inevitably of internalizing the oppressor. But mostly I rely on Mike Gold's line in *Jews Without Money:* "Every persecuted race becomes a race of fanatics." (Generally seems to apply less to women, hoary Margaret Thatcher notwithstanding.)

Permanently installed as my premiere antidote: the wonderful Harry Hay, who, with leftist friends, started the first modern, and in its inception, militant, gay organization in 1951, the Mattachine Society. (I was delighted to just read that the IWW had influenced Hay: as a young man, he'd worked summers on ranches where IWW ranch hand members introduced him to the tenets of Marxism.)

Remaining an activist, Hay separated both from the Mattachine Society and from the Communist Party when it became clear they were mutually incompatible, and both missing the mark: the former turning too assimilationist, the CP classically homophobic. (I also recently read that when he left, the CP declared Hay a "Lifelong Friend of the Party.") Later, partly as a result of his longtime interest in Native American cultures, Hay started the audacious Radical Faeries: affirming gayness as a form of spiritual calling, a unique group dedicated to balancing political work with spiritual renewal.

X1

"Go home—or else," the "Supreme Leader" told the million demonstrating Iranians (as estimated by MSNBC, the indispensable liberal cable news station) in today's silent "mourning march" to honor those who've been killed so far (God only knows how many have been arrested or disappeared) in the massive protests against their fraudulent elections. In yesterday's news conference, "re-elected" president Ahmadinejad proclaimed, "We like everyone."

Today also, an email from Greg, one of the few diehard local activists from "back in the day," calling for a sit-in in the governor's San Diego office. I've admired the commitment and tenacity of Greg and his partner, Susan, a current leader of the Peace and Justice Coalition, since '68, and the Radical Coalition years. When Susan's longtime ex, Alex, died decades ago—a genuine character and profoundly inefficient stoner/mechanic/organizer—his memorial was unlike any San Diego experience I'd ever had (of course, both were from New York): hundreds of leftists in a church reveling in war stories about this red diaper baby's somewhat dada activities in demonstrations or personal emergencies.

(Alex's least endearing appearance was as a 40-something undergrad. Rarely attending my Tactics of Pop Culture course, he'd occasionally rush into lecture hall the minute the session was over, in greasy coveralls, reeking of pot, asking, with a completely straight face: "Did I miss anything?" Assigned a group project, Alex claimed that his group would never tell him where they were meeting—I totally believed him.)

A sociology prof at a community college (we met as fellow grad students), Greg is exactly opposite of an egotist (and rather antithetical to Alex, too): responsible, bright, funny, good-natured (and good looking in the blond, SoCal way). In the last decade or twenty he's been leading the futile, low-cost

*housing battle, partly working with ACORN until its recent decimation by
the right. (San Diego has no rent control at all. On the infrequent year it gets
put on the ballot, landlords spend a fortune to convince little old ladies to vote
yes—which, naturally, means voting no. When the nauseatingly self-congrat-
ulatory city council finally passed a bill requiring 10% of new construction to
be low cost housing, they added a caveat: a small fee by which companies could
opt out.)*

Greg's email today read, in part:

> I have been an activist in progressive causes for over forty
> years, but I have never seen a crisis like we face today. Gov-
> ernor Schwarzenegger's proposed cuts threaten the health
> of nearly one million children, the livelihood of a half mil-
> lion CALWORKS recipients, and the medication of tens of
> thousands of our HIV-positive brothers and sisters. Leave
> aside the facts that these cuts mean giving up millions of dol-
> lars in federal matching money, they are deeply immoral.

*In Obama's six months or so in office, he hasn't been able to undo much of
anything that Bush destroyed. Officially, the economy is improving slightly:
unemployment figures are down—everybody's already lost their jobs! Meanwhile: countless empty storefronts, foreclosed houses, bankrupt chain stores,
small businesses shut down or reduced to miniscule size, life savings and IRAs
depleted.*

*Now it appears that Obama's much vaunted health care reform will be
seriously watered down; a miracle if any kind of decent public option will be
passed. Single payer was never really on the table, Obama recently terming it
"radical." Witness so many Democrats deep in the insurance companies' pockets. To conceal that pathetic truth must be why Obama keeps pointlessly calling for bipartisan support from the utterly hostile Republicans. It may well be,
too, that he's a centrist who prefers compromising to fighting. (In retrospect,
but only in retrospect, bully Hillary is looking mighty fine!)*

*California is rapidly sinking: unlike most other states, the bottom nowhere
in sight. How can the already eviscerated UC system retain its "world class"
status?—the state's last claim to be cutting edge, now that gay marriage was
abolished while some Eastern states, and even Iowa, have instituted it. Both*

the UC and Cal State systems are frantically raising tuitions, slashing enrollments, lowering salaries: "work furlough" being an only slightly less Orwellian phrase than "jobless recovery" (especially at UCSD where the "furloughed" are permitted to neither cancel classes nor close their labs).

Top academics have been turning down jobs here, bailing, retiring. SDSU and UCSD both have indefinite hiring freezes of faculty and staff. Nor are they replacing anyone: attrition, the name of the game. Huge holes are quickly appearing in departments' curricula: offering fewer and much larger classes will then justify devious administrators further consolidating and eliminating programs and staff—due to demonstrable lack of student demand, of course. The decimation of the humanities seems to be an inevitable, and ultimate, goal at science-heavy UCSD.

Community colleges are jam packed and cut to the bone. Schwarzenegger, who evidently doesn't give a fuck about education or human beings, has just proposed eliminating the entire category of student CAL grants. Heartening to see large, statewide student protests last spring, but they're manifestly hopeless: downsizing and privatizing "public" higher education are clearly policy decisions coming from way on top.

My own job at UCSD feels relatively secure for awhile (SDSU less so): they need somebody to teach something, and thanks to past, hard-fought union battles, they can't easily replace us continuing appointment lecturers with younger, cheaper ones. Even during the era when part time faculties were burgeoning everywhere, it was an arduous battle to gain any kind of niche in the system since passing my Ph.D. exams, and never writing a thesis (having never aspired to be a scholar)—didn't get health benefits till I was in my 40s, or a contract at UCSD that ensured them for another 15 years.

Anything can happen in the next few years. If I were ten years younger, or five, I'd be an anxious wreck. Now, if they get rid of me, I'm vested, however slightly, in the pension system, and thanks to the union will most likely be eligible to retire with medical benefits, with Joe, my domestic partner, keeping his; I could already get some Social Security, and Medicare isn't too far down the line.

All this engendered anxiety begs for a more cooperative sensibility to emerge—teams, among extended families, groups of friends and exxes: recall-

ing past fantasies, and even some realities, like food co-ops and print collectives. Unlikely, but the best we can hope for.

Actually, when I met Greg, and Susan and Alex in '68, my first year in grad school, the Radical Coalition hadn't yet come into existence. Ad hoc, somewhat amorphous groups would plan demos at school or try to coordinate when Berkeley called for strikes. At a particularly frustrated point during the ever-escalating war, we cooked up the dumb idea to block the train which carried war materials to the north: a maneuver that had been tried various times in northern California, resulting in at least one protestor's legs being chopped off on the tracks.

We chose Del Mar, a bourgie suburb where I and lots of students lived. (Many were kicked out for jacked up summer racing season rentals, but our alcoholic landlord lived on the other side of the rundown duplex. The price of our ticket to ride: hoarse litanies of despair, shouted *at any time, day or night...SHIT!! SHIT!! GODDAMN MOTHER NATURE! SHIT! Later, we learned that his father was a Chicano worker on the railroad who had bought this piece of land in 1904: Ignacio, trapped in paradise.)*

Having sent out the call to local groups, hundreds of protestors showed up, and about twice as many cops who gleefully chased us through the placid streets of Del Mar—up the hills, onto the beaches—clubs a swingin': arresting several students who made a bonfire on the tracks. Activists from all over town were furious at our disorganization. Duh! We realized we needed a cohesive group with stronger ties to the rest of the anti-war movement here.

One of the bonfire starters (I was his TA) was planning to go to medical school, and was terrified that his career would be over before it ever began. Luckily, his father's lawyers managed to plea bargain down the charges. At David's trial, it came out that the D.A. had a tape recording of the initial meeting which maybe a dozen of us had stupidly held at school, in the Revelle College "Informal Lounge"—fortunately for David, he wasn't there.

They probably had planted a tape recorder, and were watching from a nearby building (most likely, the "Formal Lounge!"): their transcripts didn't identify any conspirators by name; instead, they used Homeric epithets, like "the little Jewish guy with thick black glasses." (Not me, incidentally; mine are rimless: F, a friend who'd come from Harvard to grad school here with Marcuse. Despite his brilliant rationalism, F had been on the Central Committee of the Progressive Labor Party on the east coast: he and his girlfriend quitting this Maoist sect when they realized how deeply out of touch its leaders were with what was going on in any actual workplace which they fancied they were organizing.)

XII

Reynolds claims that, chiefly, black writers and thinkers have championed John Brown. Langston Hughes declared that the Civil War began with his raid, and that he is "one of the great martyr names of all history and the men who fought with him rank high on the scrolls of freedom."

I was startled to discover Langston Hughes' close ties to Brown. His maternal grandmother had been married to two of Brown's followers: Lewis S. Leary, a runaway slave, died at Harper's Ferry, and Charles H. Langston came close to joining the raid. Leary was hanged with his free born nephew, John Copeland, who had also left Raleigh, North Carolina to study at Oberlin, then the most progressive college in the country, and an important stop on the Underground Railroad.

Oberlin's administrators and faculty were mostly proponents of immediate emancipation, and the town had the distinction of never losing a fugitive slave to federal agents. A large group of abolitionists had been indicted there shortly before Leary and Copeland attended an anti-slavery rally in Cleveland, with about 10,000 people, resulting in their joining John Brown. Leary had participated in the Oberlin rescue: when a black man was seized by two slave-hunters, an angry group of black and white collegians and residents snatched the fugitive from his captors and hid him.

W.E.B. DuBois' classic 1909 biography of Brown sets a eulogistic tone. Providing useful information, particularly about the positions of other abolitionists, black and white, towards Brown, DuBois also documents the 1830s when decades-old Black laws, generally supported by whites in the

North, suddenly began to be enforced to reduce burgeoning Negro populations: no Negro was allowed to settle in Ohio unless within 20 days he could give bond of $500 signed by two bondsmen who would guarantee his good behavior and support; there were stiff fines for harboring a fugitive; no Negro was allowed to give evidence where a white man was party.

DuBois mythicizes Brown, apparently following the man's own lead. Brown had once told Frederick Douglass, for example, that God made the Alleghany mountains as a haven for escaped slaves. DuBois writes:

> In the Alleghanies John Brown was all but born; their forests were his boyhood wonderland; in their villages he married his wives and begot his clan. On the sides of the Alleghanies he tended his sheep and dreamed his terrible dream. It was the mystic, awful voice of the mountains that lured him to liberty, death, and martyrdom within their wildest fastness, and in their bosom he sleeps his last.

Reynolds points out that decades later important figures revered Brown. Eugene V. Debs, the socialist who ran for the U.S. presidency 5 times between 1900 and 1920 stated, "The greatest hero of them all was John Brown…(who) when the cross came, stood forth almost alone and struck the blow—the immortal blow that put an end to the most infamous of human institutions—slavery." Likewise, Clarence Darrow "worshipped Brown." In a 1912 speech before the Radical Club in San Francisco, he said, "No sordid motive ever moved Brown's life; his commander was the great Jehovah, and the outcome was determined since the morning stars sang together and the world was new."

In 1975, the Weather Underground published a journal called *Osawatomie* (site of Brown's Kansas massacre), and in the late '70s, a Southern organization, the John Brown Brigade, made several deadly attacks on the Ku Klux Klan. Admittedly, there's quite a down side to Brown's brand of martyred individualism: his name has also been invoked by several right wing nuts who bombed abortion clinics, as well as by the infamous Timothy McVeigh whose Oklahoma City federal building bombing killed 168 people.

Soon after its formulation, the Radical Coalition participated in planning the first city-wide, anti-war march downtown, with a rally in the park: sitting on the floor and stairs in an old Victorian house, a large group representing organizations all over the region; a considerable number of us didn't know each other, or who to trust, but we did know we'd need to work together seemingly unto eternity . . . and that there were a number of agents in the room.

Two days later, fellow grad students Carol, Jeff and I crashed a party at the home of a haute bourgeois Marxist prof in Del Mar (his wife was to become a very successful literary agent), given for a visiting French feminist, Christiane Rochefort. Although, in our experience, this couple had never been to any kind of organizing meeting in their lives, the guy started criticizing the demonstration from an "objective" perspective.

Too many speakers! Because the group members were more or less strangers, we explained, each one wanted to make sure their own messages got out there. Besides, the rally was in the park on a beautiful day, so its length was irrelevant. We didn't touch on the agent issue, or everyone's relative degrees of paranoia about what they could even say at that meeting. Nor did we bring up the lengthy discussions about how to entice the media: could we manage to have the representative of the liberal National Council of Churches speaking at the precise moment they showed up (as opposed to some wild-eyed, perpetually photogenic hippie)?

Nonetheless, this "armchair Del Marxist" insisted his objective observer perspective was both requisite and correct. Carol (now a dean at Columbia), and Jeff (former arts editor at the Village Voice *and* Philadelphia Inquirer*) started raising their voices. Soon several people were shouting—rather incongruous in those swanky digs. Just as the dust was settling, the hostess turned to Ms. Rochefort, and declared: "Can you imagine? You invite them into your home, and this is how they behave!" First of all, they hadn't invited us; worse, of course, she was invoking the highly demonized "private property" prerogative.*

What a hubbub! Christiane Rochefort grabbed the 3 of us, taking us out to the backyard. Gazing up at the night sky, sweetly pointing out various constellations, she chatted about which ones were visible in France that time of year. It seemed as though she'd been through hundreds of situations like this before.

X111

A number of significant activists have closely identified with John Brown: Mother Jones was known as "John Brown in petticoats," also "the most dangerous woman in America." (I think she and Emma Goldman vied for the latter title, until they deported Goldman back to Russia, where she was not amused, and didn't tarry.) In crusading for the United Mine Workers, Mother Jones made frequent references to abolitionists: carrying a well-worn volume of Wendell Phillip's anti-slavery speeches with her everywhere.

When faced with the issue of violence in the labor movement, she often invoked John Brown's name to show how visionaries were reviled as fanatics then vindicated as heroes. In his brief introduction to the first edition of Mother Jones' *Autobiography*, a polemic more than an accurate account of her personal history, Clarence Darrow wrote: "Like John Brown, she has a singleness of purpose, a personal fearlessness and a contempt for established wrongs," and, like him, she is uncompromising, seeing right and wrong as clear-cut which is precisely the source of her courage.

The sharp contrast between Mother Jones' self-styled, sweet-faced, grandmotherly appearance and that raw courage—braving Pennsylvania winters, West Virginia mountains, armed thugs, and prison guards—"never failed to arouse awe," declares her biographer, Elliott J. Gorn. Her power as a dramatist—the national press often referred to her as a guardian angel or Joan of Arc—involved the way she juxtaposed images: sacred motherhood and mass marches of women, black Victorian dress and speeches of hellfire.

Sometimes traveling with a band and phonograph, she'd read from the Declaration of Independence, and miners' contracts, and tell strikers that the czar of Russia would be dethroned if he attempted to force such tyranny on his subjects. Often organizing women into apron wearing, "mop and bucket" brigades who would march for miles to confront and intimidate scabs, Mother Jones would also convince local farmers to donate food and lodging to strikers and their families.

Between 1897 and 1904, the strikes Mother Jones helped the United Mine Workers win in the coal wars of West Virginia and Colorado enormously improved the standard of living, safety, and family life of miners. In 1905, about 675,000 American men dug coal: nearly three quarters of them working at union scale, 300,000 being UMW members.

On the payroll of the Socialist Party of America for a decade as a speaker, Mother Jones viewed her battles as part of an overall socialist agenda (even after she left the Party) to deal with the exploitation of labor inherent in capitalism: strikes of the steel workers and streetcar industries, Milwaukee breweries, Arizona copper mines, New York city garment workers; defending Mexican revolutionaries and imprisoned labor activists like Tom Mooney who was sentenced to death for allegedly bombing a San Francisco Preparedness Day parade in 1915. (Both United Railroads and Pacific Gas and Electric company officials openly advocated using perjured testimony to frame militants like Mooney.)

Susan and Alex (and Greg) and I were part of the opposition to Stalin's emissary here on earth—in the form of Jésus, brought to the Farm Workers support group meeting by one of its CP members in order to force the expulsion of the 2 lone, mild-mannered Trots from our group. (As far as I know, liquidation was never on the table.)

There had been a fracas in Coachella Valley: strikers were about to confront scabs coming out of the fields, just as some Trotskyites started handing out their own newspapers. Everyone's attention was diverted to this internal struggle, and the scabs slunk away, unexcoriated for the day. We were already aware this ongoing issue was not trivial: all media not put out by the UFW had been banned in the Valley.

Jésus's credentials were unclear. However, he was heavily muscled, with lots of what looked like prison tats, long straight dark hair, red bandana, menacing glare. He stood there stolidly, tight-lipped, powerful arms folded across expansive chest, as we argued against him—I took a rather high-handed (and high-pitched!) this-is-too-ridiculous-to-even-discuss approach.

We prevailed in a vote: fortunately, this group did not attempt to run by consensus, which meant meetings lasted less than half a day. (We only had a few CP members or fellow travelers. Most of us had been thankful that, previ-

ously, this kind of sectarianism which we'd heard so much about in cities like Boston had not been very divisive in San Diego.)

After the vote, Jésus muscled up to me, and muttered darkly, "Dirty Trot!"

"Even worse," I replied snarkily, and somewhat untruthfully. "I'm an anarchist!"

Walking out, a timid soul (the most dubiously straight of the 3 straight men in the Radical Coalition that I would eventually have sex with—once each) who did identify as an anarchist whispered in a paranoid tone that I should never utter the A word to a Stalinist; who knows what might happen!

Oy! I did not respond.

Actually, I had been *drawn to anarchism ever since reading Emma Goldman's autobiography: especially the kind where they work with organically evolving groups that sort of self-dissolve after accomplishing the specific goals for which they were created.*

Sometimes I had to belie those sympathies: for instance, the Radical Coalition had planned publicity around our occupying all the seats in a room where a military recruiter was scheduled to speak. Just as the guy appeared, R, a colorful, renowned, and somewhat crazy German lit prof and writer bopped him over the head with a rolled up magazine.

Of course, the administration, and local right wing Copley press jumped on it, happy to deflect attention away from the issue of military recruiting on campus. Although I thought R's act was kind of funny, and clearly in keeping with his own self-professed anarchist leanings, I was charged with writing a statement for the North Star, *the alternative paper we were putting out.*

(Really, Bill and Leslie, my roommate, and longtime friend, were writing, with the help of Liberation News Service, and laying out the paper with little assistance. I sometimes contributed collaborative cultural critique columns with friends, under the pen name "Marlene Zamora." Leslie, a.k.a. "Knute Hotchkiss," was also studying Chinese at the time—we all did learn to meet deadlines, and to work outside our comfort zones.)

My article dutifully chided R's individualism as counter-productive to effective organizing. I remember when I read it aloud to the RC, everyone applauded except the person I most respected: M, another of those 3 straights (but that rendezvous happened years later), a brilliant physics grad student (son of a physicist), and dedicated Trot, who'd come from Harvard via a year in prison for burning his draft card. (Unimaginable to me, considering the many accessible anti-war shrinks in Boston, ever ready to certify insanity for one and all. I myself was pre-certified, having started therapy in high school—not a moment too soon.)

Years later, some students made a "citizen's arrest" of Professor R (universally thought to be a major coke head) while he was spray painting anti-Reagan graffiti on one of UCSD's horrendous new concrete bunker classroom buildings. The press had a field day!

XIV

Mother Jones was the only woman present at the secret 1905 Chicago convention where the inspirational International Workers of the World was founded: their goal, industrial democracy; to seize power in a "bloodless revolution" through direct action, and ultimately a general strike. Their concept of "one big union" remained a forthright challenge to the craft-oriented AFL locals, while the IWW motto "an injury to one is an injury to all" contrasted the more mainstream Knights of Labor "an injury to one is the concern of all." IWW free speech movements (often declaiming about awful conditions in primitive migratory camps) in conservative cities like Spokane and San Diego provoked intense prosecution. (When Elizabeth Gurley Flynn was arrested in Spokane, she discovered that one local prison was being used as a brothel by policemen and sailors.)

This IWW convergence, along with Eugene Debs' consolidation of several left factions into a socialist party, blended well with a tradition of fiercely anti-monopoly American populist sentiments, originating in the Farmers' Alliances of the 1870s and '80s. Some populists sought to restore pre-corporate, rural- and small-town America, but the Populist (or People's) Party also emphasized mass participation in organizing and decision making, and included committed socialists who supported government ownership of basic industries. Many of its members had been influenced by Edward Bellamy's enormously popular, utopian socialist novel, *Looking Backward*.

A definitive split occurred: the IWW eschewing electoral politics, and the Socialist Party distancing itself from IWW sabotage tactics. At one time, the Party had 100,000 members and 1,200 office holders in 340 municipalities. Its *Appeal to Reason* was the country's leading radical newspaper by 1900, and perhaps its most widely disseminated political weekly, with circulation peaking at three-quarter million subscribers in 1913. Debs got 900,000 votes for president in 1912, while in prison. Divisive opinions about the First World War decimated the Socialist Party; the Wobblies took no official position, though, of course, they opposed all capitalist wars.

"Big Bill" Haywood, my other favorite IWW, and Western Federation of Miners, leader was completely destroyed once President Wilson launched a full-scale attack on the IWW in 1917, viewing them as promoting anti-war sentiment and sabotaging war production. One morning, Justice Department agents raided Wobblie offices in every city in the country, seizing everything they could find, from correspondence and typewriters to desks, rubber bands, and paper clips, confiscating over five tons of material from the Chicago office alone.

Haywood had previously emerged from jail, where he'd read Marx and Engels, as an international celebrity; in a highly publicized trial (for which Mother Jones was a major fundraiser), his brilliant young lawyer, Clarence Darrow, got him acquitted of trumped-up charges of planting the bomb which had killed former Idaho governor, Frank Steutenberg, a notorious union buster. Haywood had then met with European leaders like Rosa Luxemburg and Lenin, and used his fame to reach large sectors of unorganized workers, including Pacific northwest "timber beasts," hobo harvesters, itinerant construction workers, racially excluded east and southern European, black, Mexican and Asian farm workers.

But his health had been deteriorating—with diabetes and ulcers, he'd always been a hard drinker—and he watched fellow prisoners being carted off: one died, and one went mad. While out of jail on bail, between appeals, new charges were filed against him carrying a possible 30-year sentence. Haywood skipped bail, and took a boat to Russia. An activist, not an ideologue, he found himself with nothing to do there, never learning the language; near the end he married a Russian working woman who spoke no English. Haywood died several years later, sick and lonely, an official Soviet state hero.

This is how the agent "Bill King" reappeared: I first met Jack, my on-and-off-again-for-years boyfriend (he was on and off practically everyone in town, including a wealthy La Jolla matron who periodically whisked him away to her lair in Positano!) at an orgy at school, on occasion of their tearing down the Anomaly Factory: water tower turned multimedia theater by a group of incredibly innovative students who had pulled together a sophisticated computer lighting and sound system. The school was inaugurating its official Theater Dept. which initially was very square.

Jack, who had just gotten out of County Mental Health that day, was in the pitch black orgy room they'd set up for the bash—after some bodily contact, I crawled out, and waited to see what he looked like. When he emerged, we joined in painting psychedelic designs on the inside walls: very few people weren't on acid.

Jack (long dead) was an excellent artist on SSI, and had a great, cheap loft space in downtown San Diego where I started hanging out. Fascinating in its pre-gentrification heyday, downtown was full of sailors, hookers, greasy spoons, tattoo parlors, bars, dirty book stores, welfare hotels, scattered artists. After the bars closed, locals would regularly come out to sit on the bus stop benches, nodding and lazin' on the banks of the meandering Mississip'. (Many years later, the city replaced some with extremely uncomfortable metal benches, then tried to electrify them, as an anti-vagrant measure, resulting in at least one death.)

I was already co-editing a magazine of San Diego writers and artists, CRAWL OUT YOUR WINDOW, and was starting to do performances (happily abandoned a few years later, having glimpsed how much I had to learn, by collaborating with composers and video artists); so organizing a downtown artists group to showcase local visual artists and performers seemed a natural way to feel more connected to a community that I could help to cohere: mostly outside of the schools, I hoped, where I was starting to teach as an adjunct.

The United Artists Coalition (I was president) lasted a couple of years, until Jack lost his space to developers: putting on visual arts and multi-media shows with large, appreciative, culturally deprived audiences—with no grant money or outside support at all, though I was still spending a lot of time writing grants for the magazine. (Two wonderful friends, Ron Robboy and Sanda Agalides, also came out of the UAC.)

Community Arts was forming downtown then, co-founded by the nefarious J, long vilified by the left all over town: a poverty pimp. Whenever there was a trickle of money for alternative education, women's services or the arts, she and her "collective" would rapidly move in to set up a do-nothing agency which would garner all the funds: paying themselves salaries to run their own bureaucracies.

Now they were after Carter's CETA money, and their project was to renovate a building slated to be torn down in a year: so they paid some carpenters and construction people—and, of course, themselves, to administer a basically non-existent arts program. We got a lot of media attention by opposing them, calling for CETA money to be used more like the WPA—to pay artists to make art in public places—which, we were quick to point out, was already happening in more progressive cities. (Jack was warned several times on the streets of downtown San Diego, by seedy looking men, to stop using his studio as an organizing site.)

Lynn T. was very helpful: a newly arrived, savvy anarchist who moved from town to town, causing as much havoc as possible—her 20-something, sweetly effete, apolitical gay son in tow. Lynn applied for a CETA job with Community Arts, and when she was turned down, brought a discrimination suit against them which we made sure was well-publicized. (While the local media was right wing, they also fed on controversy—and had little to report on regarding the arts here.)

The more we investigated J, the worse it got. Every activist woman in town that I trusted (including Susan) believed J was an agent. A number of key women in grassroots groups and alternative spaces had gotten together to publish an extensive, thoroughly documented account of the history of the collective's activities: while not concluding in print that she was an agent, they did argue that even if J were only an opportunist, she had a seriously pernicious effect on community organizing. The amount of time and attention they'd put into this document clearly indicated how much of a threat J constituted. I began to distribute this white paper to allies at UCSD and SDSU.

Then we discovered that Community Arts' cofounder, also a J (J2) had recently breezed into La Jolla with her new husband, a former D.A. who, several years earlier, had prosecuted and closed the best independent bookstore in town for selling Henry Miller's novels. J2 appeared to be a vaguely liberal-ish, rich charity lady, with lots of Sacramento connections.

XV

Before ever becoming a union organizer, Mother Jones endured hell: embodying one paradigm of what it takes to create a lifelong activist. Gorn believes that "tragedy freed her for a life of commitment," and that her "witness against the horrors visited on the poor by the rich was energized by a need to expiate her own survival." At age 14 or 15, Mary Harris' family left Ireland during the potato blight which killed over a million people within 5 years, about 12% of the Irish population.

The Irish saying, "God created the potato blight, but the English made the famine" was a response to heartless policies underscored by a long-held belief about Irish sloth by political conservatives and evangelical Protestants. They evicted those who couldn't pay the landlords, denied relief to any peasant renting even a quarter of an acre of land, and demolished homes across the country to consolidate farms.

Death was omnipresent, due to diseases like scurvy and dysentery.

At the town of Skull in County Cork, an English midshipman came ashore and watched a crowd of 500 half-naked people waiting for soup. A local doctor told him that no one would be alive in three weeks.

Mary's family migrated to Toronto where she went to public school and teachers college, then taught in a convent school. Rarely seeing her family once she left home, Mary first became a dressmaker in Michigan and Chicago, then a teacher in Memphis in 1860. There, much of the unskilled labor was performed by the Irish or blacks, and one of the ugliest race riots in American history occurred in 1866. For 3 days, Irish police and firemen led the way in terrorizing African Americans: 46 were killed, 200 shot or beaten, 5 raped; the mob burned 89 homes, 4 churches and 12 schools. The next year, a Memphian founded the KKK.

Mary and her husband George Jones were not among the proletariat: as a schoolteacher, she reached the top (albeit a low-paying one) of the occupational ladder for Irish women, although most schools would not employ mothers. An iron molder, George Jones was part of the aristocracy of labor—foundry work was a highly skilled trade, and Jones was a member of the International Iron Molders Union which had established substantial control of the industry by the end of the Civil War.

The family lived in an Irish neighborhood on one of a few blocks of freestanding houses lying, unfortunately, between two forks of a bayou: an open cesspool that became stagnant in the summer and flooded in the rainy season. An epidemic of yellow fever devastated Memphis in 1867, a gruesome disease which had come west from Africa with the slave trade, mostly hitting the poor who couldn't afford to leave town.

Mary Jones' husband and 4 children all died of the fever, one by one.

Rather than focusing on her personal losses, her *Autobiography* emphasizes an increasing awareness of the callous "luxury and extravagance" of the rich. Returning to Chicago and dressmaking, just 4 years after her family's deaths, during an unprecedented drought, she lost all of her belongings in the great Chicago fire. The unfounded rumor of Mrs. O'Leary's cow kicking over a gas lamp because she sought revenge for being dumped off the relief rolls due to fraudulent claims deepened the widespread stereotypes of the Irish as a "dangerous class." The depression of 1873 and rebuilding of Chicago further solidified worker-capitalist antagonism—at the age of 34, first joining the Knights of Labor, Mary Jones was ready to turn to activism.

Oh! about the agent, "Bill King": In our investigation of J and her notorious circle, we learned that at a series of open meetings at their house—where King was living at the time—he'd called for bombing the KOGO tower, a local TV transmitter. Wow! A decisive moment in our strategizing—pull out all the stops!

Several years after King had been exposed and vanished, J's household tried to become its own chapter of the New American Movement: the already existing San Diego chapter threatened to quit en masse; I notified two friends in the east who were close to Richard Healey, one of NAM's founders and publisher of In These Times, specifically regarding the known agent's KOGO tower provocations. The J collective was not permitted to join NAM, and seemed to fade away after that.

One of NAM's local leaders, Nick Nichols, was a saint: an associate professor at State (he didn't publish so the English Dept. never promoted him), and major union activist there (we often collaborated after I'd been elected by the part-time faculty as their advocate). Nick worked tirelessly for medical benefits for part-timers and a host of other causes which didn't directly impact his own life. In his 50s, Nick had a heart attack and died while driving on the freeway. Afterwards, everybody said oh yes, of course, we all knew he had a bum ticker—actually, that terminology wasn't much used—but he would never slow down. Viewing him as a martyr, they were all anticipating an early death.

Apparently, Richard Healey had to fight his mother who had been courted by J's group: Dorothy Healey was an admirable, former officer of the California Communist Party, and well known as "the Red Queen of LA" from her Pacifica radio show. She left the CP in the '70s (rather late, I'd say, having futilely tried to reform it from within, after Khrushchev's famous 1956 speech, finally denouncing Stalin), and wrote a compelling autobiography about her lifelong commitment. Dorothy became a major supporter of NAM because its concept was decentralized, autonomous but linked groups of socialists.

After Community Arts was demolished, one of its bureaucrats (who in no way was part of "the collective"), Lynn Schuette, a fine painter who became a friend, decided to start Sushi, an artist's run, alternative downtown gallery/performance space, and asked me to be the board's first vice-president. (Just last week, Sushi closed its doors after 3 decades of almost continual operation—personally, I'd lost interest in it and in performance art long long ago.)

Most of the original board were not artists, except for Philip Galas (avant-garde vocalist Diamanda's talented and charming brother), who was the first person, and one of the youngest I ever knew, to die of AIDS, but professional administrators at local museums and university art galleries. I continued writing grants, booking local talent, and advocating for more public arts and literature funding—though, alarmingly, Sushi often paid less attention to the locals' tech needs than to promoting mini-stars they were importing from New York and San Francisco.

These mostly likable board members were competent at sucking up to rich people. I thought I could pick up a few techniques, but a couple of years was more than enough to convince me to forget it: my attitude toward the wealthy was too belligerent, and entitled. Thus ended the career of an erstwhile activist, unable to derive enough satisfaction even with fellow cultural workers. After that, it was about consistently showing up at demos—until many years later, that, too, seemed fruitless.

XV1

Before Sushi, "liberal" had basically signified people you tried to squeeze a lot of money out of so they could alleviate their bourgeois guilt. But some of those administrators were clearly committed to the arts and also, understandably, wanted to make a decent living. They countered my archetypal image of "do-gooder" J2: glib, over-dressed, monstrous La Jolla Community Arts lady. Today, of course, everything has disastrously moved so far to the right that "liberal" sounds like a badge of honor, especially when that word comes out of the mouths of Tea Party idiots—or at least it connotes someone who isn't *totally* greedy and solipsistic.

My personal tastes still run toward those who are nauseated unto death with capitalism, *and* care about enfranchising the poor, or, minimally, are leading Bohemian, anti-materialistic lifestyles; I also appreciate Hollywood iconoclasts in the James Dean mold. His filmic rebellions were always striving for greater authenticity: trying to overcome alienation to be recognized by peers, and mainly family, for who he was, not who they needed him to be. (That he himself could do this with his madam mother was key to *East of Eden.*) In *Rebel Without a Cause,* Natalie Wood, and Sal Mineo agree, in a rare peaceful moment, that sincerity is the most important quality—a suitably ironic anthem of the bad boy/outsider celebrity age which they all were so instrumental in shaping.

In any case, it's evident that here and now at least, nobody, particularly politicians, can do much to fight the cartels (and their lackeys, unwitting or otherwise), though that raises the question of whether Obama is even trying. Looking back at Chicago, the most progressive city in the country in the late 19th century (partly due to the radicalizing effects of the Haymarket Square police riot)—with its enormous immigrant population, gifted leaders and five newspapers in three languages promulgating anarchist ideas—it seems clear that some of the most effective individuals were, indeed, liberals who managed to crack open seams by working (in) the system: especially women, like Jane Addams (later awarded the Nobel Peace Prize), founder of Hull House, a key center of Chicago's intellectual and political ferment.

A major facility with numerous buildings in a multi-ethnic, immigrant neighborhood (at one point counting 36 nationalities in their ward), Hull House provided limited cooperative housing, health care, a day care center, library, savings bank, kindergarten, gymnasium, concerts, dances, theater featuring children's plays, Ibsen and Shaw, and many works in native tongues (even Sophocles in ancient Greek), gardens, clubs for new mothers, studios and classes in arts, crafts, photography, English language, U.S. citizenship, and Extension classes in conjunction with the University of

Chicago which prompted them to become the first school to offer sociology as a discipline.

Addams towed a classic liberal line. Deeply involved in the fight for labor legislation (placing great faith in the principle of arbitrators) and government regulation of labor practices, and against unscrupulous unemployment agencies and job contractors, she was much more ambivalent about strikes: rueful that the public identified her with even the most radical wildcat strikes which she didn't endorse. As a fundraiser, she often had to refuse "tainted money" (a hot button issue in that period) from owners of sordid sweatshops essentially bribing her to abandon advocacy work: embarrassing the settlement house's Board of Trustees who had originally solicited the donations.

A keen pragmatist, candid in her fascinating, if somewhat stilted, *20 Years at Hull House,* about many obstacles, such as parents who abused their own children—forcing them to work in factories to support the family, because they brought in more money than their (olive picking) father's unskilled labor, sometimes taking all their wages, so the children ended up in court for petty thievery—Addams helped install members of her organization, the Juvenile Protection Association, to work as sympathetic parole officers. Although drawn to "that gallant company of socialists"—"I saw nowhere a more devoted effort to understand and relieve that heavy pressure than the socialists were making"—she also felt they were too dogmatic.

Hull House featured popular weekly debates, often between leftists like Lloyd George and social reformers, and hosted individuals like Upton Sinclair, Benny Goodman, the British statesman Ramsey MacDonald, W. MacKenzie King who became Canada's prime minister. Full of praise for the "wonderful procession" of Russian revolutionaries who spoke there, particularly Peter Kropotkin, "doubtless the most distinguished," still Addams viewed her main allies as humanists, Ethical Cultural societies, settlement house workers in Britain, and trade unionists: insisting that reformers not ideologues ultimately effected social change.

Trained at the elite Rockford Seminary for Women, adamant that educated women not retreat from the world after school, Addams attracted other strong women to Hull House. She herself never married, and shared her life for 37 years with Mary Rozet Smith. One Hull House resident, Florence Kelley, ran the Consumers League, dedicated to abolishing child labor and advocating for the poor; she was appointed the first factory inspector in Illinois. Like Addams, born into a rock-ribbed Republican family, Kelley was a Marxist who translated Engels, and later became a socialist. (Naturally, Republicans ain't what they used to be: both Jane Addams and her father revered Lincoln.)

Safety codes finally piqued national attention with the 1911 Triangle Shirtwaist factory fire in which 146 women, mostly young Jewish and Italian workers, were burnt to a crisp, locked in that rattrap. Frances Perkins, who witnessed the fire, worked at Hull House after graduating from Mount Holyoke, and went on to become the first female Cabinet member: FDR's Secretary of Labor, architect of much of the progressive New Deal legislation. Before that, Perkins had been picked by former president Teddy Roosevelt, then appointed by Governor Al Smith to head the New York State Factory Investigating Committee, a completely new kind of government watchdog entity.

Mother Jones (decidedly *not* a liberal) had taken a job in a Southern mill for a close look at child labor, and had organized a well-publicized march of striking textile workers' children from Philadelphia to New York. Frequently sharing a platform opposing child labor with Kelley, and Jane Addams, she never publicly recognized the work of these middle class women. (Somewhat oddly, Mother Jones also didn't support the suffragette movement: viewing women as exploited workers who would one day leave their miserably paying jobs to become homemakers and mothers, their husbands earning a living wage.)

It would be easier to feel sanguine about the simplest formula, that both radicals and liberals have been crucial in improving people's lives, if everything didn't seem to be careening so out of control now, toward financial and environmental catastrophe. If, say, oil hadn't been spilling into the Gulf of Mexico for over two months with nobody appearing to have a clue about how to stop it.

Obama, who continues insanely amping up the Afghanistan war, makes an occasional speech while the oil cartel BP has taken out many TV ads assuring us that they won't rest easy till this disturbing situation is made right! (Last week, the CEO was caught on video, yachting in the Mediterranean.) One ad features a pained yet determined looking black executive on the beach, gazing firmly straight ahead—not into the ever-darkening sea. These men are personally concerned, you see.

The Tea Party people, who appear to now be the Republican Party, have repeatedly apologized to this CEO guy. When they're not too busy expressing delight at Arizona's fascist governor passing what amounts to a mandatory racial profiling law which the federal government has finally decided to challenge in court. In a further nod toward imbecility, Arizona has also banned ethnic studies courses from the schools. Gleefully spewing all the racism that was slightly held in check before the election, because it seemed to embarrass Republican hopeful McCain who today is a total Tea Party toady.

MARGARET SANGER IN WEST PALM BEACH

The scene: Mel's parents' condo in Florida, circa 1999.

The players: Mel visiting his parents; his father has Parkinson's, somewhat out of it. Cousin P visiting her mother, Belle. Mel's mother and Belle are sisters. They basically hate each other. Cousin P and her mother also hate each other, and rarely converse.

The occasion: It's Cousin P's 62nd birthday; she's drinking. Mel's mother has made dinner and a cake. After dinner, Cousin P blows out the candles, and there's the usual (very) light conversation, when suddenly....

> **P:** You know, Grandma liked to give blow jobs!
>
> SILENCE.
>
> **P:** She told me that Grandpa used to go down the block to the _____ *(insert Yiddish word for prostitutes)* because grandma didn't know how to give blow jobs. She asked me how.

Mel's father looks like he's about to hit Cousin P or fall off his chair. Mel notices that Cousin P uses a lot more Yiddish words in Florida than she ever does at home in California.

SILENCE.

P: You know grandma had two abortions.

SILENCE.

Mel (in a neutral tone): Well, that's possible. Margaret Sanger *did* open her birth control clinic in Brownsville—right near them.

SILENCE.

Mel: And it mostly served Jews and Italians.

SILENCE.

P (to Mel's mother, rather belligerently): Didn't grandma ever talk to you about sex?

Mel's mother (curtly): NO. And I'd like to keep it that way.

Father shoots P murderous glance.

SILENCE. CURTAIN.

XV11

Marcus Rediker's *THE SLAVE SHIP: A Human History* is a grim account of the conditions on the "floating dungeons" or "portable prisons" which carried 12.4 million souls over almost 400 years of the slave trade, producing a "yield" of some 9 million Atlantic workers who survived longer than a year. His sources are mainly first-hand, written accounts from seamen or British captains, who usually kept extensive logs: some repentant, others not, some published as pamphlets by abolitionist societies. *(Wonder if John Brown had access to any of them.)*

Slave trading demanded such a concentration of resources that private capital could not originally finance it, but beginning in the early 18th century, so-called free traders triumphed over the regulated monopolies, like the Royal African Company. It's estimated that 80% of the captains sailing out of British ports came from commercial backgrounds. A few had fathers who were merchants; some were descended from ship captains. Most were sons of waterfront artisans: connections leading to the captain's cabin, only after considerable sea experience.

"The captain bullies the men, the men torture the slaves, the slaves' hearts are breaking with despair."

Often, the sailors had been sent to jail by tavern keepers for debt, then bailed out by ship captains who paid their bills and took their labor, simply exchanging one prison for another. Captains ordered the sailors to commit vicious behavior: forced feedings, whippings, casual violence of all kinds, compelling slaves to exercise ("dance") in shackles, to maintain their health and value as commodities. Although some sailors signed on to gain unrestricted access to the bodies of African women, the same hardware of bondage used on the slaves—manacles and shackles, neck irons, chains, branding irons, thumbscrews, cat o' nine tails—could also be inflicted on insubordinate sailors, victimized in many ways.

A 200-ton ship that required a crew of 35 to handle 350 enslaved people would carry a cargo of sugar (or ballast) back to home port, needing only 16, perhaps fewer, men. If not enough sailors died toward the end of the Middle Passage, just as treatment of the enslaved began to improve, to ready them for market, the captain started driving the crew hard, in the hope that some would desert when they reached port.

A substantial number were in such bad health by voyage's end that they could no longer work: suffering from malaria, ophthalmia, "Guinea worms" (parasites that grew to enormous size, usually in the legs), and various ulcers. In the West Indies and Jamaica, one seaman reported that they "were lying on the wharfs and other places in an ulcerated and helpless state." "Used in a barbarous manner," and bilked of their wages, they sometimes crawled into empty sugar casks on the docks to die.

The austere distance which captains maintained from slaves ("command isolation") was facilitated by the ship's construction: the captains' quarters were as far away as possible from the hold, whose design, of course, was the forerunner of our own modern day sardine tin. However, when it came to punishing mutinous slaves, captains personally took charge, often vying for reputation as the worst bully: "they studied, with no small attention how to make death as excruciating as possible."

This book is replete with gruesome examples: typically, the captain would only whip and scarify the most valuable slaves; others "he used to create terror." Captain Harding, for example, killed one mutinous slave "immediately, and made the others eat his heart and liver." One woman "he hoisted up by the Thumbs, whipp'd and slashed her with knives before the other slaves till she died."

Captain John Newtown, who wrote the song "Amazing Grace," famously had a change of heart, publishing influential abolitionist pamphlets, and testifying to the House of Commons committees. But in letters kept from public scrutiny, he documented some of the worst abuses he'd either heard about, witnessed or participated in (it was usually unclear which). Newton described Captain Richard Jackson "jointing" his slaves after a failed insurrection:

> that is, he cut off, with an axe, first their feet, then their legs below the knee, then their thighs; in like manner their hands, then their arms below the elbow, and then at their shoulders, till the bodies remained only like the trunk of a tree when all the branches are lopped off; and, lastly their heads.

Throwing the reeking members into the bulk of the chained slaves on deck, Jackson then proceeded to a second group condemned to death:

> He tied round the upper parts of the heads … so loosely as to admit a short lever; by continuing to turn the lever, he drew the point more and more tight, till at length he forced their eyes to stand out of their heads; and when he had satiated himself with their torments, he cut their heads off.

Rediker describes sharks' feeding frenzies when slaves jumped overboard (despite these ships being built with an extra wide girth as a deterrent to suicide). After one slave killed himself, a futile search for his weapon resulted in actually looking closely at the dead man: finding blood on his fingertips and "ragged edges around the wound," they concluded that he had ripped open his throat with his own fingernails.

Many cruel capitalist twists. Once the forests of New England were thinned out for shipbuilding, southern pine was mostly used—so "the ships brought the laborers and the laborers cut the wood to make the ships." Officers were given bonuses in the form of their own "privilege slaves"—bought with the merchants' capital. (A ship captain might get 7 privilege slaves, a chief mate 2, a doctor 1.) In addition, even sailors often had the option of shipping their slaves for personal sale, with no cargo charges.

Among the most heinous policies were those of the insurance companies—surprise, surprise! A major scandalous atrocity in the history of slavery was reported by John Newton: in 1781, Captain Luke Collingwood sailed with a crew of 17 and a "cargo" of 470 tightly packed slaves from West Africa to Jamaica. Soon, sixty Africans and seven crew members died of an illness. Collingwood told his crew that "if the slaves died a natural death, it would be the loss of the owners of the ship; *but if they were thrown alive into the sea, it would be the loss of the underwriters.*"

That evening, over some protests, the crew threw 54 slaves, hands bound, overboard; another 42 two days later, and 26 more soon afterwards. Watching the hideous spectacle, 10 more slaves committed suicide by following suit. Later, the case was tried in court when the insurer refused to pay and the owners sued in response; Collingwood pretended a lack of water had caused his actions.

Gordon was recently in the hospital for a week. When I visited him, he said he was okay, because "I caught it early this time"—whatever that means. On his way home from being discharged, he bought a bottle of vodka, according to Marcia; within a day he was coughing blood and back in the hospital. When they released Gordon again, they suggested he sign up for hospice care.

I was just over there on Gay Pride Day: significant because we went to the first marches together in the '70s, when they were fun! People strutting down the streets, shouting their lungs out. I have some great photos of Gordon there—young, twinkling eyes, mouth wide open: what an awful contrast to his present cadaverous look.

Joe and I have been avoiding the marches for a long time, they're so corporate: every business rep and lame politician in the area riding in long cars, waving vacuously (not to mention all those beautiful, untouchable studs on the bars' floats). Nobody can even march unless they're in an officially recognized contingent; $20 to get into the "festival" (beer garden/dance floor). I usually try to at least be with gay friends (a sadly diminishing pool) that day if I haven't contrived to get out of town. No way Gordon will still be here this time next year.

XV111

One book I haven't read yet, *SLAVERY BY ANOTHER NAME*, apparently goes into excruciating detail about the huge rise in black convict labor after the war: a dimension not usually discussed in the history of slavery. I *have* been reading Eric Dean, Jr.'s impacting *SHOOK OVER HELL*, which compares post-traumatic stress after Vietnam and the Civil War. A contemporary classification, of course: most of the Civil War vets were diagnosed, weirdly, with "nostalgia" or homesickness; in WW1, the term was shell shock. In both cases, the chief medical strategy was to get them back onto the battlefield as rapidly as possible.

Dean's research, particularly in archives of the Indiana State hospitals, reveals numerous dysfunctional Civil War vets committed years after the war ended, when families could no longer cope with their paranoia and disassociation. Moving anecdotes abound: there's the vet who ate constantly for years, feeding tramps all day long, staying up all night cooking pies and cakes to put out for birds and stray dogs. His daughter testified that, "he could not bear to see anything that seemed to be hungry."

> **DERANGED CIVIL WAR VET:** He told me he was going home to cut off his wife's head and use it for a ball in a bowling alley.

The book also features firsthand accounts of daily wartime life: marching for thirty miles a day in the heat, sometimes for weeks in a row. Men would throw away blankets, overcoats, even knapsacks, and still become violently ill from the exertion: some vomiting repeatedly, having convulsions, dying from heatstroke.

Dean vividly describes combat conditions. Smokeless gunpowder had not yet been developed, so after the firing began, the battlefield was frequently overshadowed in a pall of smoke and sulfurous vapors; the dreadful pounding and concussion from the cannons was such that blood gushed out of the nose and ears of one infantryman at the Battle of New Hope in Georgia; many soldiers were permanently deafened. Exhausted survivors often fell asleep atop mounds of corpses.

Without affirming the visionary powers that W.E.B. Dubois sees in John Brown, it seems perfectly reasonable to view Brown as giving his life trying to deflect massive carnage and misery, or maybe to accelerate its conclusion. *(Could he have believed there was any chance of Harper's Ferry succeeding—or of his escaping? Maybe he imagined a martyrdom which would trigger longer term positive effects. Or was this mostly just a final NO in the face of depthless greed and cruelty?)*

> I John Brown am now quite *certain* that the crimes of this *guilty, land will never be* purged *away; but with Blood.* I had *as I now think: vainly* flattered myself that without *very* much Bloodshed; it might be done.

Where did Wobblies get the courage or fortitude to fight out-and-out class warfare?: against Pinkertons, labor spies, state militias controlled by robber barons whose fortunes mainly originated with Civil War profiteering, selling shoddy, often defective goods to both North and South.

At least the Wobblies had each other—for ranting, consolation, partying. Could any of them have clung to shared delusions that the IWW would win in the long run? Maybe the fight itself was enough—until they were thrown in jail, deported or drafted along with all WW1 dissidents who despised the war as a genuinely insane manifestation of international imperialism.

Basically, the courts have always been in the hands of the ruling class: after anti-trust acts were passed, the Supreme Court simply nullified them,

by declaring that corporations were persons, thus their money was protected by the 14th Amendment (initially intended to protect newly freed
slaves, of course). As Howard Zinn points out, the primacy of "private
property" went back to the Founding Fathers who had learned their law in
the era of Blackstone's Commentaries: "So great is the regard of the law for
private property that it will not authorize the least violation of it, no, not
even for the common good of the whole community."

The recent Supreme Court decision allowing corporations unlimited
spending on political campaigns is merely the latest embellishment of this
criminal policy.

Republican governors and legislators in many states are trying to strip
public sector union workers of the right to collective bargaining: currently,
Wisconsin's Democratic state legislators are holed up in a motel across the
state line, preventing a quorum from being reached, giving press confer-
ences, stating they won't be coerced into voting for such a retrograde bill.

Most of the other states gleefully moving toward disenfranchising poor
voters, like requiring official identification at the polls, have a majority without the Democrats, and are poised to further wipe out the middle class.

XIX

It's not like I can derive optimism from looking at past rebellions. The
future seems so bleak, with no basis for the economy: no manufacturing
left; no protective tax incentives or tariffs in place, to even start rebuilding
it. *Free trade reigns; all fall down.*

I don't imagine becoming involved in any community work
again—though if I could afford to retire…? Teaching, despite chronic
complaining about workload, has offered enough contact and sense of
being useful, along with trying to be a good (but not overly caretaking)
friend.

*Nevertheless, these magnificently defiant figures from the past who dedi-
cated their lives to improving the common good, remain crucial: oddly personal, familial, immanent*—despite knowing how easy it is to idealize them,

abstracting icons from the mess of egos, repression and conflicting ideologies which constitutes realpolitik.

Not that I had ever aspired to be like them: if anything, my goals concerned doing wholeheartedly and thoroughly whatever felt most compelling at any given time—creatively, intellectually, politically—rather than following the dictates of careerism or anybody else's agenda.

Still, if hope exists, for me, it's somehow there, in history: I've been steadily reading and writing in this vein for more than a decade.

Sustaining partly *because* so much is still not visible, yet to be explored: so many names heard intermittently, echoing, resonating, surfacing, strangely interconnected, as people's lives are. Promising further materializations of a stellar, worldwide heritage—directly antithetical to our mandated dog-eat-dog brutality: most conspicuous in the proud old tradition of not guaranteeing inhabitants health care, let alone basic rights to food and shelter. *(The pursuit of happiness, anyone?)*

Who knows what these rebels suffered? What types and depths of communities were they able to establish as home?

How often did they resort to imitating the living dead for camouflage? Crying "daddy," "mommy!" in panicked and bored crowds, so that nobody would suspect—perhaps not even themselves—that they, profoundly, didn't need those others to define themselves.

The wonderful Walt Whitman's epic Song of Myself *ends:*

> I bequeath myself to the dirt to grow from the grass I love,
> If you want me again look for me under your boot-soles.

> You will hardly know who I am or what I mean,
> But I shall be good health to you nevertheless,
> And filter and fibre your blood.

> Failing to fetch me at first keep encouraged,
> Missing me one place search another,
> I stop somewhere waiting for you.

MEL FREILICHER

is a longtime San Diego resident who was publisher
and co-editor of *CRAWL OUT YOUR WINDOW*
for 15 years, a magazine of regional literature and arts.
Freilicher's previous book, *THE UNMAKING OF
AMERICANS: 7 Lives* was published by SD City
Works Press, and he was anthologized in their *SUN-
SHINE/NOIR: Writing from San Diego and Tijuana.*
Also anthologized in *Contemporary American Fiction*
from Sun and Moon Press, and *Performance Anthology:
Source Book for a Decade of California Performance Art*
by Contemporary Arts Press, Freilicher has chapbooks
out from Standing Stones Press and Obscure Publica-
tions. His reviews, essays and fiction have appeared
in many publications, such as *American Book Review,
Fiction International, San Diego Free Press, SD Union-
Tribune, Central Park, Frame-work: Journal of the LA
Center for Photographic Arts;
Flue: Magazine of Franklin
Furnace Archive, NYC; River
Styx, Fourteen Hills, Golden
Handcuffs Review, eye-rhyme:
journal of experimental litera-
ture, Rampike, BIGBRIDGE.*

Photo: Joe Keenan

Freilicher has been teaching creative writing in UCSD's
Literature Dept. for several decades.